W9-ACC-469

TOKEN OF DARKNESS

Also by Amelia Atwater-Rhodes

DEN OF SHADOWS
In the Forests of the Night
Demon in My View
Shattered Mirror
Midnight Predator

THE KIESHA'RA
Hawksong
Snakecharm
Falcondance
Wolfcry
Wyvernhail

Persistence of Memory

TOKEN OF DARKNESS

Amelia Atwater-Rhodes

DELACORTE PRESS

FRANKLIN COUNTY LIBRARY
906 NORTH MAIN STREET
LOUISBURG, NC 27549
BRANCHES IN BUNN,
FRANKLINTON, & YOUNGSVILLE

This is a work of fiction. Names, characters, places, and incidents either are the product of the author's imagination or are used fictitiously. Any resemblance to actual persons, living or dead, events, or locales is entirely coincidental.

Copyright © 2010 by Amelia Atwater-Rhodes

All rights reserved. Published in the United States by Delacorte Press, an imprint of Random House Children's Books, a division of Random House, Inc., New York.

Delacorte Press is a registered trademark and the colophon is a trademark of Random House, Inc.

Visit us on the Web! www.randomhouse.com/teens
Educators and librarians, for a variety of teaching tools, visit us at www.randomhouse.com/teachers

Library of Congress Cataloging-in-Publication Data is available upon request.

ISBN: 978-0-385-73750-0 (trade) — ISBN: 978-0-385-90670-8 (lib. bdg.)
ISBN: 978-0-375-89597-5 (e-book)

The text of this book is set in 12-point Requiem Text.
Book design by Trish Parcell Watts
Printed in the United States of America
10 9 8 7 6 5 4 3 2

First Edition

Random House Children's Books supports the First Amendment and celebrates the right to read.

Token of Darkness is dedicated to two individuals who shall remain unnamed here, whose passing strongly inspired this story. One was very dear to me, and one was a complete stranger. So many people move in and out of our lives, often affecting us in ways we do not fully recognize or understand. By extension, we can never realize what effect we have on others, even those we have never met.

That being said, Cooper's story owes thanks to:

My editor, Jodi. Her insight has been invaluable these past eight years as we have worked together to refine Nyeusigrube and the stories within, from the golden age of shapeshifters in the Kiesha'ra Series to the modern Den of Shadows.

My agent, Tom. I don't know what I would do without him. Probably curl up in someone's basement, writing stories no one would ever read and occasionally wondering if I was supposed to get a royalty statement at some point.

My fellow writers and my tireless beta-readers—especially Mason, who did a sixteen-hour-long session of beta-reading "boot camp" when I was panicking about how I could revise the first-draft mess I had on December 1 into an actual novel. Thank you to Bri, Zim, Ria, and Shauna, and to my sister, Rachel, for her support when I was preparing the revisions for submission.

The Office of Letters and Light; all the individuals and groups responsible for National Novel Writing Month (nanowrimo.org); and Bri, ML to Nyeusigrube. In 2006, NaNoWriMo helped me get past the worst writer's block I have ever experienced; NaNo07 produced Cooper. 30 days. 50k. Hurrah!

Deep into that darkness peering, long I stood there wondering, fearing,
Doubting, dreaming dreams no mortal ever dared to dream before;
But the silence was unbroken, and the darkness gave no token,
And the only word there spoken was the whispered word, "Lenore!"
This I whispered, and an echo murmured back the word, "Lenore!"—
Merely this and nothing more.

Back into the chamber turning, all my soul within me burning,
Soon again I heard a tapping somewhat louder than before.
"Surely," said I, "surely that is something at my window lattice;
Let me see then, what thereat is, and this mystery explore—
Let my heart be still a moment and this mystery explore;—
'Tis the wind and nothing more!

Open here I flung the shutter, when, with many a flirt and flutter,
In there stepped a stately Raven of the saintly days of yore.
Not the least obeisance made he; not a minute stopped or stayed he,
But, with mien of lord or lady, perched above my chamber door—
Perched upon a bust of Pallas just above my chamber door—
Perched, and sat, and nothing more.

Then the ebony bird beguiling my sad fancy into smiling,
By the grave and stern decorum of the countenance it wore.
"Though thy crest be shorn and shaven, thou," I said, "art sure no craven,
Ghastly grim and ancient Raven wandering from the Nightly shore—
Tell me what thy lordly name is on the Night's Plutonian shore!"
Quoth the raven, "Nevermore."

—from "The Raven," by
Edgar Allan Poe

PROLOGUE

The darkness was alive, and it was hungry. Cooper didn't know how he knew that, but he did, the way he knew things in nightmares: it was hungry, and it would devour him if it could. The shadows twisted like vines and snapped like dogs at his heels, solid enough to menace but not enough for him to struggle against them.

He had been lost, and then the darkness had risen around him, and now he couldn't find his way back.

At least the shadows weren't focused on him. They had other prey. He needed to get somewhere safe before they noticed him again—before they turned their attention away from the girl.

The shadows had torn her apart. She was shapeless, faceless, as she struggled with them. How had she come to be there? The air seemed to weep for her, the mist coalescing into heavy drops of rain.

Insanely, he dove forward, trying to chase away the creatures that harried her. They nipped at him, but as he tried to close his arms around the girl and help gather her together, he felt himself being *yanked* backward, into a shell that was too small to fit inside.

An explosion of lights and noise told him he was awake. He opened his eyes to find the girl there, fighting with the shadows that still surrounded him. She clawed at them with her hands until they faded into the corners of the room.

Trembling, she reached out to touch his cheek.

"Necromantic golem."

Cooper gave a start. He had been lost in reverie, the content of which had fled his mind the moment Samantha had spoken.

"What?"

"Necromantic golem," she repeated. "I'm just saying. It's an option."

Cooper looked down, and realized he had nicked himself with the knife when she startled him. The cut wasn't bad, but he pulled his hand and the knife away from the counter and the compulsively neat apple slices sitting there.

"You're going to have to clarify for me," he said as he washed the cut and reached for a bandage. "And get off the counter."

"I'm not technically *on* the counter," she objected, "and I should think it would be the natural answer to our situation."

Cooper shook his head and studied Samantha as he carefully cleaned up after his mishap.

She was petite, standing only a little over five feet tall. She had straight blond hair with silver highlights that looked natural, along with a few streaks of teal that didn't. She was cute, actually, bordering on sexy, a fact that did not seem to be lost on her. Today she was wearing a short, pleated skirt—black with neon pink splotches—and a green and orange striped peasant-style blouse. Beneath the skirt, she wore gray paisley stockings, torn at the bottom to expose most of her bare feet.

Her eyes were . . . well, it was hard to tell. They were prismatic. Looking in them almost gave Cooper as much of a headache as today's outfit did.

Cooper had asked Samantha about her clothes at some point over the summer. She had told him she didn't decide what to "wear"—her clothes were no more solid than she was—but admitted that she "liked bright colors." Very bright, apparently.

She certainly *looked* like she was sitting on the counter, but of course it didn't matter. She could as easily have been standing *in* the counter, or on the wall or the ceiling. She did things like that sometimes, defying the laws of physics without seeming to notice or care.

If she had been alive, it probably would have been

considered a health hazard when she walked through the food, but since she was a ghost and not dripping ectoplasm, it was only annoying. And only to Cooper, because no one but him seemed able to see her. Even when she lay in the middle of the pastries display case as if it were Snow White's glass coffin, everyone else was oblivious to her presence, including Cooper's father, who owned the shop.

"Seriously," she insisted now, apparently not ready to let this idea drop. "Golem."

He rolled his eyes. "I assume you mean for you."

"Uh-huh."

"And I assume you mean I should make one, so you can . . . take it over, or whatever."

"It's not possession if it's a golem, since they don't have souls, right?" she said, making him wince at the way her voice echoed when she got excited. "And it's not a zombie or anything since you'd be making it and not using a dead person."

"You wouldn't be able to sit on the ceiling anymore if you actually had a body," he pointed out.

She paused, chewing her lip, then shrugged, and fell halfway through the counter before finding her feet on the floor. "I wouldn't be able to sit on the ceiling, but I'd be able to . . . to curl up on a cold night, wrapped in a blanket, with a mug of raspberry hot cocoa. So, what do you say?"

"I say I don't know how to make a golem, necromantic or otherwise."

"You use clay, duh!"

"Where do you *get* this stuff?" he asked. "Clay. Okay. And *then* . . . ?"

"Then . . . then . . . *I want a body!* I'm sick of this non-corporeal crap. Check out the library's occult section. Check out *Harry Potter*. I don't *care!*"

With the last outburst, Samantha flickered like a candle flame going out and disappeared. Cooper shrugged and turned back to see if the apples were salvageable. He wasn't worried about Samantha. She often disappeared, and always came back.

Maybe he should have been concerned about *himself* since he was the only person who could see her, but he wasn't. He knew better than to tell anyone else about her, though; they would probably lock him away in a padded room somewhere. Could he really blame them?

The fact of the matter was, he was being haunted by the color-coordination-challenged ghost of a teenage girl. She had appeared by his bedside when he had woken in a hospital last July, and neither of them knew why.

He finished cutting the apples and started laying them into tarts. The work was soothing, mechanical. His father was in the next room, kneading bread dough; occasionally, his soft humming reached as far as this room, but mostly it was quiet, the way Cooper liked it. He appreciated the routine of waking up at four in the morning, getting to the shop by four-thirty to bake bread and pastries and brew the coffee before they opened at seven. Then—at least on weekdays, like today—he hung up his apron as his father spoke to the first of the morning's customers, rolled down his sleeves, and trudged fifteen minutes to school.

Before this summer, he would have laughed at the guy he was now: quiet, reserved, and living very much in his own head, instead of constantly surrounded by outgoing friends who only managed by sheer luck not to get kicked out of every public place they entered.

It was only the fourth day of his senior year of high school. It was going to be a long year, and not because the day started when he had already been awake for more than three hours . . . often longer. . . .

The problem was, he couldn't find it in him to *care* about this year. He used to care about things, people. His room, his stuff. His friends, especially the other guys on the Lenmark Ocelots football team, including John, who had been his best . friend since sixth grade. He had barely seen any of them since the end of the previous school year. Then there was his car, a 1993 Dodge Colt hatchback—more than a decade old with more than a hundred thousand miles on it, but it rode like a dream, like *his* dream, like freedom.

Cooper didn't have that anymore, either, and he didn't miss it, even yesterday, when he had walked from his father's coffee shop to school in a fine drizzle. His father had offered to let him take the family car, but he hadn't minded the cold or the rain or the way it made Samantha sparkle as it fell through her.

Necromantic golem. Maybe he should look into that. How, he wasn't at all sure. He didn't know if Samantha's idea was

7

possible, but then again, he didn't used to believe in ghosts. He knew a few people at school who claimed to be witches, but most of them seemed to be more about earthy religion or pissing off their parents, and he was pretty sure they would respond negatively if he asked them if they had any recommendations for how to deal with the undead.

He probably shouldn't start at the school library, either. That seemed like a good way to get pulled into the counselor's office for an emergency meeting.

"Cooper, you're late," his English teacher announced as he walked through the door, and slipped to the back of the classroom.

"Sorry," he mumbled, and reached in his bag for his copy of *The Color Purple,* only to realize he had left it at home that morning. His teacher shook her head with a sigh before turning back to discussing the book.

Cooper's mind wandered. Necromantic golem, indeed. Maybe he could start with myths?

Why was he focused on this, of all things? He wished he could help Samantha, but the bottom line was, she was dead. He had watched enough horror flicks to know that if you wanted to help a ghost, you did it by telling them to go into the light, or helping them let go, or whatever. You didn't do it by making them new bodies; that was the way to B movies and red corn syrup.

Maybe he should talk to a priest? He didn't know any, but his mother went to the Unitarian Universalist church. Or were ghosts more of a Catholic thing?

He jumped violently when someone's cell phone rang across the room, a screaming jangle of noise. His chair skittered backward and crashed to the floor, turning all eyes his way.

"Sorry," he said again. He pulled his chair upright and sat back down, trying to hide the fact that he was shaking and sweating, and his heart was racing so loudly he could barely hear the people around him murmuring comments. Across the room, he saw John mouth the words, "Are you okay?"

He nodded, then hunched down lower in his seat and picked up a pen to pretend to take notes.

"Okay, everyone, quiet down," the teacher said. "Put your books away. We're having a quiz."

The whispering turned to grumbled protests. Cooper just shrugged and put away the notebook he hadn't yet opened. He hadn't read the book past the first couple of pages, but that was fine. Samantha reappeared after the quizzes were handed out, and reported on the variety of responses from around the room, noting which were most common and so were more likely to be right.

It wasn't a good way to start the school year, but if he was going to be haunted, he might as well get something worthwhile out of it.

"I think I've read this book," Samantha announced as the quizzes were collected. The idea seemed to excite her. "No, I'm almost *sure* I've read this book! I remember it! I mean, I remember what it's *about*. But I don't actually re-member *reading* it."

She sounded deflated. Cooper fought the urge to groan.

The problem with helping Samantha resolve whatever issues were tying her to this world was that she had no memory of *who* she was, just random details that may or may not have been from her previous existence. She didn't know why she was relegated to this half-life, without the ability to touch or affect anything in the world. She remembered snow despite not having seen it since her death, and sometimes remembered books or movies. She didn't have a heavy Boston accent, so probably wasn't from the city, but she could easily be from any other area of Massachusetts. She was also obviously well-versed in movies, especially horror movies. She knew her own name in the same way; she was certain she was Samantha, but couldn't recall anyone but Cooper who had ever addressed her that way.

She and Cooper had sat at the computer for hours at a time this summer, reading all the obituaries for the area in an attempt to find out who Samantha might be. There had been deaths in the accident that occurred immediately before Cooper had met Samantha, but none that felt right to her. And not just because they were men.

They didn't even know if her physical description would mean anything. Her basic coloring, height and age usually remained more or less constant, but everything else seemed to change from one manifestation to the next. Samantha said she had no conscious control over it.

After spending most of the month of August searching, they had kind of given up as Cooper had prepared to return to school. So far as Samantha was concerned, she had been born that July, at the moment when Cooper had woken in the hospital.

He knelt down to slowly put his notebook away at the end of class, using it as an excuse to avoid his classmates as they filed out, and so was surprised when he looked up to find a 227-pound linebacker hovering above him. He slammed his head against the desk leg as he tried to stand up.

"Damn it, John!" he shouted, rubbing the spot he had just banged. "You scared the hell out of me."

"I had to sneak up," John answered. "You run faster than I do."

Cooper fumbled for words while fighting the urge to do just that—bolt. "Look, man, I'm sorry—"

"No big," John interrupted. Then he winced. "I mean, of course it's—" He broke off, and shook his head.

Cooper shut his eyes for a moment and drew a breath, trying to figure out something to say that would help them to get past this. Neither of them wanted to acknowledge that the "big deal" they were both avoiding talking about had to do with Cooper spending most of the summer in the hospital following an eight-car pileup on the highway the first weekend after school let out in June. It had to do with the fact that, in the blink of an eye and the flash of brake lights, he had gone from being John's best friend to someone even *Cooper* barely recognized.

When he opened his eyes, though, John wasn't alone. The black mist from Cooper's nightmares seemed to have risen from the floor. It rippled and crawled up John's body, twisting around his limbs like something alive. John didn't seem to see the shadows, but his skin rose in gooseflesh, and he crossed his arms as if he was cold.

Cooper looked to Samantha, hoping for some kind of reassurance—even hearing that he was hallucinating, and the dark creatures weren't real would be comforting at this point—but she had backed into a corner and was kicking at them. They didn't seem to be able to hold on to her, but they stalked around her, snarling.

John took a step back from Cooper, averting his gaze with an awkward expression. "Anyway," he said with a shiver that dislodged two of the creatures that had been hunched on his shoulders. "I just wanted to see how you were doing. If you're not up to hanging out, that's . . . that's cool, I guess."

"John—"

John nodded as if in response to something else, then hoisted his backpack more solidly on his shoulder and backed hurriedly out the door, nearly knocking down a freshman trying to get in for the next class.

The shadows receded into the corners of the room, fading into something harmless. Cooper grasped the desk until his heart stopped pounding, and then he looked up at Samantha, whose form seemed tattered, the colors from her hair to her paisley stockings all a little less bright.

"I thought they were gone," she whispered. "I haven't seen them since the hospital."

Cooper just stared at her, not knowing how to respond. He had not known that she had ever seen the shadows before, but had thought they were part of his private fears. He had once had a nightmare about a living, creeping, hungry darkness, like a swarm of locusts made of smoke and misery. When he woke, Samantha had been beside him.

2

Cooper made it through his next couple of classes using a combination of willpower and despair. He didn't know what else to do. As soon as lunch came around, though, he rushed from the school building. As a senior with no history of discipline or academic problems, he had off-campus privileges, so no one looked twice as he walked toward town.

Samantha chattered nervously as Cooper wandered, finally deciding he should force himself to eat something. He hadn't had breakfast, and it would be a long time before dinner. Besides, it gave him something to do other than search the corners for those *things*.

"I would kill for a BLT," Samantha declared as she sat on the table at the deli while Cooper ate. She now seemed to be dressed in faded, torn jeans with dribbles and splashes of paint in a vast variety of colors, a baggy T-shirt sporting the image of a pink elephant, and a large gray sweatshirt with the zipper torn out and the sleeves cut off just above the elbows. Her earlier fears seemed forgotten. "Seriously. If I could taste anything . . . if I could *eat* that would be the first thing I would get."

Cooper's nerves had settled enough that he was finally able to focus on her and respond. "How do you know you're not a vegetarian?" he asked, speaking quietly so his voice wouldn't carry. Thankfully, the sandwich shop was so busy, he figured people wouldn't notice that a few stray words belonged to a one-sided conversation.

"I can remember what bacon tastes like, and it is *goooooood,*" Samantha replied. "I'm no veggie. Have you given any more thought to what we talked about this morning?"

The burst of laughter behind him was normal enough not to even draw his attention, but the way it abruptly cut off *did*. It seemed like an hour passed in complete silence before a familiar voice said softly, "Hi, Coop."

He tensed, his spine seeming to fuse into a lead bar, and it took a monumental effort to turn his head to face the head of the Lenmark cheerleading squad.

"Delilah, hi."

Cooper tried to make the words seem welcoming and warm, but they came out flat. He and Delilah had never been very close, but she was part of what had been Cooper's crowd. They all usually ate at the pizza place

20222831

down the street, so Cooper hadn't expected to see them here. He hadn't considered Delilah, whose social circle wasn't limited to the athletics department. In addition to cheering, he knew she built sets for the drama department and spent much of her free time in the photography lab's darkroom.

He stood up and flinched as his hip gave a sharp twinge, a pain that shot from his toes up to his shoulder. The injury from the accident didn't bother him too much anymore, but sometimes it stiffened when he sat.

For now, he stood before Delilah and felt every inch of his diminished self. She looked, as always, like she had walked right out of a magazine, in designer clothes that suited her strong and lean figure, honed by time in the gym and on the field.

With Delilah were two other girls; both looked familiar, but Cooper knew neither of their names.

"We thought we would get some lunch," Delilah said, which Cooper thought was fairly obvious. She leaned against the back of a chair as her friends went up to the counter to order food, and sighed before saying, "I've missed you, Coop. I called a couple times, but your cell always went straight to voice mail."

Since Cooper hadn't ever charged the phone his mother had bought to replace the one destroyed in the accident, he imagined he had more than a few messages.

"Who's she?" Samantha asked, moving to the middle of the table to avoid being jostled. Cooper still didn't understand why Samantha couldn't walk through people or other living creatures. He had seen some people shiver, or brush the place where their skin touched Samantha, ' but they almost never even glanced in her direction.

Delilah, however, looked up as if she heard something. Her gaze went right through Samantha, so it was obvious she couldn't see the ghost, but nevertheless Samantha gave an excited hop and said, "Hello?"

Delilah looked like she was about to say something else, but at that moment one of her friends returned and asked, "Who's this?"

"Oh." Delilah glanced quickly at where Samantha stood, then shook her head and answered. "Cooper Blake. He's from the team. Hey, get me a basil-mozzarella sandwich with bacon, then let's eat outside."

"It's all wet—"

"It's sunny," Delilah interrupted, "and I'm sure it's dry enough. Cooper will join us if he has the time." She reached out to touch his shoulder gently before adding, "Take care, Coop." She tossed her hair and walked directly outside without waiting for another word.

Well, that was weird. Cooper and Delilah hadn't exactly been best friends, but in his experience girls were usually more aggressive than guys when it came to asking about things no one really needed to talk about, like the accident or how he was feeling since. Of course, Delilah wasn't like most girls.

He tried to just be grateful she had let him off the hook.

FRANKLIN COUNTY LIBRARY
906 NORTH MAIN STREET
LOUISBURG, NC 27549
BRANCHES IN BUNN.
FRANKLINTON & YOUNGSVILLE

She had left him with an invitation to join her, or not, and absolutely no pressure either way.

"Who was that?" Samantha asked. "Girlfriend?"

Cooper shook his head and looked through the window to where Delilah and her friends were settling on benches with their backs to him. Delilah's serial first-dates never included athletes.

"Did she hear me?" Samantha asked. "She did, didn't she?"

Cooper began packing away his lunch. "She probably heard something across the room."

"Or she heard *me,* and didn't want to look crazy asking about it. You should talk to her."

"We're talking about *Delilah,* Samantha. She's a cheerleader who occasionally spends time with artsy kids. She's cool, but she's not the type to be able to do something *no one else* can."

Delilah tended to be charming overall, ruthless when someone crossed her, but generally distant. Of everyone in his normal group of friends, he shouldn't have been surprised that she was utterly unperturbed that he had simply disappeared for months.

"Coward," Samantha said. "Why don't you just—"

"Shut *up,* Samantha!" he snapped, this time getting a few odd looks from other people in the shop.

Samantha pouted, and then turned around. "I'm going to hang out and see what they say."

"Knock yourself out," Cooper mumbled under his breath, before she sauntered through the wall and back

18

toward the other girls. Cooper picked up his bag, threw out his trash, and left without looking back.

Halfway to school, he changed his mind. His hip still hurt a bit, but his doctors had told him that walking was good for him. He was willing to risk a little soreness, if it meant avoiding another run-in with old friends.

"Shouldn't you be in school?" the town librarian asked him as he approached the front desk.

"I'm at Q-tech," he answered, naming the local vocational-technical high school. He *had* nearly gone there with John, despite his parents' objections. Who wouldn't want a chance to learn stuff like computer programming and auto mechanics, after all? The deciding factor hadn't actually been his mother's horror, but the fact that John had wanted to keep playing football, and Q-tech didn't have a team. "We don't start until Monday."

"Oh." She still looked suspicious, but was a little more relaxed, which was good, since he needed her help to find anything useful in the four-floor building. "Are you looking for anything in particular?"

"Yeah, I . . ." He fumbled, trying to figure out a good place to start that didn't involve his saying, *I'm being haunted.* "I kind of forgot about the summer project I was supposed to be doing. It's on ghosts. You know, hauntings, myths and stuff about why ghosts stay around and what people do about them. Maybe stuff about warlocks dealing with the dead?"

"Third floor," she answered. "All the way back from the

stairs, turn left at the one hundreds. Parapsychology and occultism is one thirty-three."

"Thanks."

This time she actually smiled, as he trudged toward the stairwell.

Stairs.

Flat ground was okay, but stairs were still hell.

He must have paused for a little too long, because the librarian asked, "Something else I can help you with?"

He started to shake his head, not wanting to disclose . . . but then sighed. Now was not the time to be macho. "Do you have an elevator?"

She frowned again. "It's supposed to be for handicapped use only."

He wasn't *handicapped!*

"Never mind," he said.

"If you need the elevator—"

"No, I just realized I forgot something," he said, bluffing.

"Oh . . . well, if you do need it, the elevator's right around the corner past the copy machines," she said.

She turned back to the books she had been scanning in. He was almost sure that she was pointedly *not* looking at him. Not forcing him to say, "I need the elevator because, despite how I look to you at first glance, this body is in fact unsound and likely to betray me if I take the stairs."

He hesitated for a couple seconds, debating whether it

was worth trying to convince her that she *was* wrong, that he was just a lazy jock who didn't want to bother with stairs . . . and then he turned to the elevator. There were a lot of ways to lose your pride. This was just one of them. And it wasn't forever, even; the doctors said that as long as he kept doing the daily exercises he had been prescribed and attending his monthly physical therapy checkups, he would be good as new. Eventually.

Only two months ago, even walking had been impossible for him. *Breathing* had been an effort.

He hit the UP button, and as it lit and the elevator went *ding ding ding*, memories from the hospital started washing back. The doctors' shouting, the lights blinking and machines beeping, breathing for him—

No, no, no, no.

He ripped himself from the memory, only to see the elevator doors close in front of him. He hit the button again and the car opened immediately. He stepped inside, limping heavily now.

He didn't immediately hit the button for the third floor, though. Instead, he leaned back and shut his eyes, taking deep breaths. Where was Samantha? Her chatter was usually a good distraction.

Necromantic golem, that was his focus. That was what he had come here to look up or, barring that *exact* scenario, he intended to learn anything he could about ghosts. He doubted there was going to be any way to give Samantha a body, but if he couldn't do that and couldn't help her live again, then at least maybe he could find a way to bring her peace.

With these safer thoughts in mind, and the memories locked away again, he hit the button for the third floor. He still winced each time the elevator beeped, but it was only twice, and then the doors slid open and he was free.

3

There was someone already camped out in row 133, cross-legged on the floor, surrounded by books. At first, Cooper couldn't tell if the figure was a guy or a girl—all he could see were jeans, black sneakers, and an oversize black sweatshirt.

Cooper resisted the instinct to turn around, anticipating a grungy goth with black overlong hair, eyeliner and piercings, who would probably have way too much to say about the occult.

"Hey," he said, eliciting a start from the figure, who shoved his sweatshirt hood back in order to look up at Cooper.

Cooper's expectations turned out to be completely wrong. The guy's brown hair was short and spiky. He wasn't wearing any jewelry, and a collared shirt was just visible beneath the sweatshirt.

"Hey," he replied. "You startled me. Am I in your way?"

"I think we're trying to look at the same books," Cooper answered, feeling a little guilty about his previous assumptions. Considering the fact that *he* was now the guy who sat quietly at the back of the class, who had cut school to research ghosts, he should probably cut back on the goth stereotypes before he became one.

"I didn't expect to find anyone else here," Cooper admitted as the other guy gathered up some of the books he had spread about, making room. "With school and all."

"Q-tech," he answered briefly.

"Really?" Cooper asked, wondering if this guy was using the same excuse he was. He didn't look familiar, though, and didn't look young enough to be one of the underclassmen Cooper wouldn't recognize.

"Yes," he snapped, "people from Q-tech can *read*. We don't combust when we walk into libraries. God, I hate the way you—"

"Whoa, whoa, *not* what I meant," Cooper protested. "We *are* supposed to be in school today, so I told the librarian I was from Q-tech to stop her from getting on my case. I was just wondering if you had done the same."

"Oh." The hostile energy faded, replaced by an embarrassed-looking expression. "Sorry. I get a lot of grief from people who think only stupid people go to the vo-tech school."

"I wanted to go there, actually," Cooper admitted. "My parents said no."

"My mother doesn't really care where I go." The other boy shrugged. "I'm Brent, by the way."

"Cooper."

"You look familiar. Football team, right?"

"Last couple years, yeah," Cooper admitted. *But not this year.*

"That explains it," Brent said. "I went to a few games last season. You're the fast little guy."

Cooper couldn't help chuckling, since that was the exact description Coach used for him. At two inches shy of six feet tall, he had still been one of the lighter guys on the team. It was all right that he didn't have a lot of weight to throw around, though, since he had good hands and quick feet. Or, he used to.

"Get hurt in practice?" Brent asked.

Cooper cringed. He had gotten so used to carefully shifting his weight when he had to kneel or sit, relying on his good knee and hip, he hadn't given it any thought when he had slowly eased onto the floor next to Brent.

He just shook his head, and changed the subject. "So . . . anything good in here? I'm looking for stuff on ghosts."

Brent paused before asking, "What kind of 'stuff'? Haunted places? Poltergeists? Séances?"

"I'm kind of writing a book," Cooper lied. "This guy's being haunted and trying to figure out who the ghost is and how to help her. I thought I'd do some research."

"Uh-huh." The invented plotline apparently didn't impress Brent much. At least, that's what Cooper thought until Brent added, "You're a piss-poor liar. I don't even know you and I know you just made that up. I hope you were a little quicker with the librarian or she's probably called the truant officer already."

"You think?" Cooper sat up, worried.

"Nah. Elise is cool," Brent answered. "If she caught you at a movie or smoking somewhere she would call you on it in a heartbeat, but you're in a *library*. She doesn't care if you're supposed to be in class."

"Good to know." Amused, Cooper asked, "You're on a first-name basis with the librarian? Do you work here?"

"Work? No. Well, I volunteer sometimes. I practically live here when I'm not at school. I like the quiet." Brent looked at the pile of books around him, as if he was trying to decide which to pick up next.

"A little light reading?" Cooper asked, wondering why anyone would be doing such dedicated research before the school semester began. He wondered if he should insist he had been telling the truth about the book he was writing, or if he could come up with a better excuse.

"Light by my standards," Brent said, laughing a little. "I don't think I believe in ghosts, but figured it might be interesting to research the phenomenon. But anyway. Your ghost. More of a specter, or a poltergeist?"

"You just said—"

"Yeah, I don't believe for a minute you're writing a book," Brent interrupted. "And if you were looking up how to make arsenic or something I'd worry. But *ghosts*? It's an interesting topic for discussion, but not likely to get anyone in trouble. Now, let's start basic. Is your ghost location-bound or person-bound? Oh, or object-bound? They're all different."

"Person-bound, I guess," Cooper answered. Brent seemed like he could be helpful, and he wasn't likely to talk to anyone Cooper knew, so it didn't really matter why he was helping or what he thought Cooper needed the information for. "She goes wherever she wants, but this one guy is the only one who can see her." He debated adding something about the shadows, but his gut seemed to twist when he even thought of them.

Brent didn't notice his hesitation. "Oh!" he exclaimed, seeming more excited now. "Then your *person* might be the thing to focus on, not your ghost. Maybe he's psychic. Does he see ghosts a lot?"

Cooper shook his head. "No, this is the only ghost."

"Hmm." Brent paused, looking at the books around him. "Well, there are a lot of stories about people who did something—a séance, or violated a graveyard, et cetera— and got haunted for that. Is your ghost angry?"

"No, just color-challenged," Cooper mumbled, recalling Samantha's outfits.

"What?"

"Never mind. No, she isn't angry, but she's frustrated that she doesn't have a body."

"So she knows she's dead?"

Cooper nodded. "Oh yeah, she knows. She's annoyed about it."

"Young or old? Unfinished business? Maybe a tragic death, murdered and dumped somewhere, and no one's found her body and she desperately wants to make sure she gets a proper burial. That's a little cliché, though. Maybe she *was* the murderer or she kidnapped someone, only then *she* died, and her victim is trapped somewhere and she can't rest until the victim dies—or is rescued. That would be a cool story."

"Do you write?" Cooper asked.

"Nah, I'm not creative," Brent replied, straight-faced. "But your ghost—"

"Doesn't remember who she is or how she died," Cooper said, before Brent could come up with another dozen scenarios. "But I think she's young, our age, and from around here."

"Huh." Brent paused again. "Amnesiac ghost. Trauma can bring on amnesia, and death has to be pretty damn traumatic. I wonder if a ghost could get psychotherapy? Or hypnotized?"

"Let's not go that route," Cooper said, trying to derail what looked like it was about to lead into another list of possible plotlines.

"Well . . . I'd check obituaries," Brent said. "You need to figure out who she is and why she might be hanging around."

"And if she's not in there?"

"Check missing persons. There are lots of places online that have officially listed missing people, especially if she's a kid. Or if you're really brave, you—I mean, your *character,* of course—can go to the police station and say something like 'I saw this girl the other day, and she looked a lot like someone I think I saw on a missing-person flyer in Boston,' and see if they recognize the description."

"And if that doesn't work?"

"Well . . . psychics, I guess, would be your next stop," Brent said. "A real psychic would be able to tell if your character is psychic himself, or if your 'ghost' is really a ghost. She could be something else."

"Like what?"

"Anything. It's your supposed book," Brent said. "Maybe she's an alien, existing on a slightly different plane of existence from us, and the passage to Earth was so traumatic she lost her memory of it and thinks she's human since she's surrounded by them. Or maybe she's a fallen angel, and all her memories of Heaven were taken as punishment for her transgressions. Or maybe she's actually some kind of demonic figure, sent to torment your protagonist, and she's lying about not remembering who she is."

"Um . . . I think she's just a regular ghost," Cooper said. "Though those are interesting ideas," he added, mostly to be polite.

"You've pretty much admitted you don't know a thing about ghosts, so how can you be sure she's just the 'regular' kind?" Brent challenged. "She doesn't sound like a regular kind to me, not if your character can see her and talk to her and she isn't angry or anything. Maybe you should stick to writing football stories."

Cooper decided not to be offended, if only because Brent had said the words with a quirked smile, the jibe meant in good humor.

"There's nothing in here about ghosts like that?" Cooper asked, waving to all the books around him.

"Not really," Brent said. "Most ghosts tend to be location-specific. They're rarely seen. Even ghosts who haunt people tend not to be very communicative outside of a séance or something. You're sure your character hasn't desecrated any graves lately? Maybe an Indian burial ground or an ancient pagan temple?"

"Pretty sure," Cooper answered, smiling despite himself. It was the longest conversation he had had with anyone but Samantha since the accident, and even if it wasn't re-motely helpful, it felt good to joke around with another *living* human being.

4

Brent regarded the guy next to him in a vaguely clinical fashion. He had recognized Cooper Blake pretty quickly as one of the receivers from the public high's football team. They had actually met once, at a New Year's Eve party last winter, but Brent wasn't surprised that Cooper didn't remember. He had been introduced to Cooper, but they hadn't talked long.

He had been surprised to be invited to the party in the first place; he and Delilah had been involved since that September, but she had shown absolutely no interest in including him in the rest of her social life before then. He hadn't been thrilled by the event, and she hadn't invited him to any more.

He would have been happy to see Delilah's school friends in small groups; he just didn't deal well with crowds, which pulsed with the scurry of other people's thoughts, most of them unfocused and indistinct like a constant background whine that only Brent could hear. There had also been a synergy of thought among the team that was deeply unsettling for an outsider, and left him feeling distinctly *outside* no matter how welcoming the group tried to be.

Cooper, on the other hand, was hard to peg. The thoughts Brent could make out were almost hyper-focused, with a kind of white noise behind them. It wasn't something Brent had heard the likes of before, which was why he had gladly engaged in the conversation about ghosts. He was curious, and the noise made by Cooper's brain wasn't offensive. Even the zinging background thoughts that shot past Cooper's more conscious ones were so quickly suppressed that they sounded like the rustling of wind chimes.

One thing Brent knew for sure was that Cooper *was* seeing this ghost he described. Whether that meant he was psychic or hallucinating, Brent didn't know. When Brent had volunteered at the local hospital for a couple weeks over the summer, he had briefly been in a room with a hallucinating schizophrenic, and it had been spine-crawlingly horrible. The things that poor man saw, the voices he heard, were so angry. They befouled his mind and the space around him, so much so that Brent had left the room gagging, his head pounding.

That was when Brent decided to finish his mandatory-for-graduation community service at the library instead. It was quiet here, especially in the summertime. People were so trained to keep their voices down in the presence of the towering stacks of books that they even instinctively kept their thoughts small, so they were like little fluttering moths in the night.

"You okay?"

It took Brent a moment to realize that Cooper had said something.

"Oh yeah, sorry, man," Brent replied. "Um . . . oh. You haven't said when this guy started seeing his ghost."

"Does it matter?" Cooper asked.

To Brent, the static at the back of Cooper's mind seemed to get louder, as did all those rapid background thoughts.

"Sure it matters," Brent said, drawing back a little from his examination of Cooper's thoughts and trying to pay attention to the words he was saying, too. It was difficult, because thoughts weren't really comprised of any one sense, which influenced the way Brent experienced them; he tended to use words like *hear,* but he could just as well say he saw thoughts, or felt them—or maybe it was a combination. "If he hasn't messed up a grave or something else to get a particular ghost attached to him, then he's either seen ghosts all his life, or something triggered it."

Cooper shook his head. "It's a recent thing."

"How recent?"

"Couple months."

More static.

"When, specifically, did it start? I mean, what precipitated it?"

Even louder. Brent started wondering if he should back down, but he wanted to know, and that meant pushing a little harder and dealing with the headache he would have later.

"He saw her for the first time after a nightmare," Cooper answered hesitantly.

"About what?"

The static rose to a roar and those gentle wind chimes became a screeching, slamming cacophony of noise, flashing lights, and panic emanating from inside Cooper's suddenly tensed body. Overwhelmed by the impact, Brent bit his lip so hard he tasted blood as he tried to tune it out.

He reached to put a hand on Cooper's shoulder, trying to calm him. "I'm sorry, man," he said. "I didn't mean to—"

Wham.

Brent couldn't begin to describe what happened next. He had just touched Cooper's arm, when Cooper looked up, his hazel eyes suddenly an eerie silver color. Without moving, without doing a damn thing, it felt as if Cooper shoved him backward, so hard he was flying through the air.

Brent tried to curl, to brace himself for the fall, for the crash of his body impacting the shelves behind him, but it didn't come.

Instead, he found himself sitting exactly where he had

been, only coughing so hard he felt like his lungs had for-gotten how to inhale. His whole body was shaking as if he was coming out of deep hypothermia, and Cooper was drawing back, looking horrified, his face gray-pale with sweat beading on his brow.

"I'm sorry," Cooper whispered. Brent could still hear those jangling noises and lights in Cooper's brain, but was too shaken to try to tune them out or to focus on them.

They were no longer alone. A girl knelt beside Brent in scene-style clothing—mismatched and torn, but artfully so. Even if she had come to complain about the commo-tion they were making, he was grateful for her presence. She looked quizzically at Cooper, who just shook his head, still backing away as the girl knelt and tilted her head as she examined Brent.

Around them, the shadows seemed to pulse. Cooper's gaze shot from one dark blur to the next, and the girl shuddered when they drew near enough to touch her. They growled and snapped at Brent.

"I'm sorry," Cooper said again. "Samantha, we should go."

"Cooper!" the girl shouted, sounding cross and fright-ened. Brent was still too dazed from whatever had hap-pened to pick up any thoughts from her.

"Wait!" Brent choked out, but Cooper just turned and dashed the other way, his limp almost hidden in his haste as he shouldered through the double doors to the staircase.

There was no use going after him, even if Brent could

have moved at that moment. Cooper didn't want to be stopped. That was okay; Brent didn't think he was ready to deal with the ex-football star again yet. He couldn't even stand.

He drew in deep, gasping breaths. He had no idea what had just happened, or if it had been Cooper's fault or his own. He was a telepath, but unlike many of the people he had spent the last year studying with, he wasn't good at recognizing or controlling other kinds of power. He had no idea what those shadow-things had been, except that they clearly weren't good.

"Can you help me up?" he asked the girl.

She jumped, and then tentatively offered her hand, with an expression of pure shock. "Are you okay?" she asked.

"Yeah," he answered, "I think so."

He reached up, only to have her whole form dissolve when he tried to grasp her hand. Cooper's ghost? But did that mean Brent had really seen her, or had she just been a lingering image from Cooper's mind? At least, once she was gone, the shadows started to sink back into the floor and walls around him.

Brent's bones felt heavy and his muscles weak. His skin was too tight, and the air he drew into his lungs hurt. He tried to pull himself up by gripping one of the library shelves, but couldn't lift his own weight.

As he waited for his muscles to stop twitching and for his body to feel less alien, he attempted to put his thoughts in order.

Cooper could see something, which he thought was a ghost—probably the girl Brent had briefly seen, after . . . whatever Cooper had done to him. What Brent was sure of was that Cooper's actions had been accidental. Cooper had seemed horrified. Brent knew what it was like to have an unusual power, but not be able to control it.

But that didn't make it *his* job to help other lost souls. He wasn't responsible for this random guy he had just met in a library. Not at all. Cooper had his football friends. More importantly, he had Delilah. This could be *her* problem.

As soon as Brent could stand, he was going to go home and forget about Cooper Blake.

Hey, can you hear me?

"Huh?" He looked around, but as best as he could tell, the girl's voice was coming from the picture on one of the books.

You saw me for a second, didn't you? Can you hear me? Please?

"I can hear you," he answered. His voice was raspy and speaking made him start coughing.

Yes! The jubilant cry made him wince and rub his temple.

"Not so loud," he managed to say.

Sorry, she said in pretty much the same tone. *But the only person I've been able to talk to in months is Cooper, and he's a nice guy but he's not very bright and sometimes he's kind of boring, and I just don't know how I . . .*

As she spoke, the excitement in her voice never

37

dimmed, but she seemed to be getting farther and farther away. She hadn't lowered her "voice" but he strained to hear her, until in the middle of a sentence she just faded completely.

"Are you still there?" he asked.

No response, except for chills up his arms.

"Hello?"

Okay, the afternoon had officially turned into something out of a creepy horror movie. With a monumental effort, Brent forced himself to his feet. He was out of this scene. No more shouting hello at disembodied voices in empty rooms for him, thank you very much. He didn't like to meddle with dark powers or witchcraft any more than necessary. He had only been researching ghosts as follow-up to a conversation with his mentor; he was perfectly happy to go through his life without ever seeing another one.

Brent was a little unsteady, but he managed to get to the stairs, and down them. The librarian gave him a worried look, and he heard her think, *Bright boy, but so quiet,* before he managed to block out anything else. Where did he park his car? He probably shouldn't be driving in this condition, should he?

Maybe he should sit down somewhere . . . maybe get something to eat. His stomach felt all tossed up, but it was the kind of unsettled that solid food sometimes helped.

Enough ghost stories for him today.

He found his way to a little nearby bakery, but by the

time he had paid for his cup of cocoa and bagel his vision was swimming. He was having trouble keeping his own thoughts focused, which meant he couldn't keep anyone else's out, either. He retreated to the courtyard nestled between the library's old and new buildings, where a bunch of Eagle Scouts had built a beautiful garden almost no one else knew about.

He sat there, nursing the cocoa and centering himself until it didn't sound like people were screaming all around him.

He remembered what it had been like when he first started hearing things other people couldn't. He remembered how horrid he had felt, when he kept accidentally stumbling across people's secrets—their wants, their fears. Their lies. Maybe it should have made him think less of other people. Instead, he had lost his faith in himself when he couldn't stop listening. It was like peering in windows at night, and seeing people's most private moments.

Even as a kid, Brent had had a knack for predicting what people were thinking or feeling. It wasn't until he was fifteen that what he had always assumed was intuition had manifested as outright telepathy, and it wasn't too long afterward that he had ended up in the hospital, completely overwhelmed. He always felt crowded, even when there were only two or three people in a room, because they were often so conflicted that their thoughts might include five or six voices each.

He had met Delilah about a year ago, after missing a

good chunk of what should have been his sophomore year of high school. She had been the first person who had understood. It had been months before he got past his blind dependence and gratitude enough to question the fact that she seemed to have absolutely no interest in spending any time with him in *public.*

Oh, God, was he *really* going to subject Cooper to Delilah's brand of help? He remembered all too well coming out of complete, terrified, helpless isolation and ending up in her hands. Yes, she had introduced him to Ryan le Coire, but she had also paraded him around like her newest project. She had put him back in the hospital for a while last spring after one of her magic experiments went disastrously wrong. He still didn't know what she had been trying to do, since she had never attempted to ask his permission or explain. They just broke up, and had rarely seen each other since.

Brent wasn't going to push Cooper to confide how or when he started seeing his ghost, and he *definitely* wasn't going to put a hand on his shoulder—or anywhere near him if he could avoid it—in the future. But he could at least keep him out of Delilah's grasp by introducing him directly to someone who would help. Ryan le Coire. While Ryan seemed at first glance like a normal guy, someone who could be a grad student, the twenty-six-year-old was actually a sorcerer. And, as Ryan put it, he was the heir to the most powerful human magics in the Western Hemisphere. Ryan had been able to teach Brent how to tune out some of the thoughts he heard, so he'd be less overwhelmed. Brent knew that Ryan didn't believe in ghosts, but he certainly would know something useful.

There was too much pain radiating from Cooper's body and mind, not to mention the darkness swirling around both him and his ghost, for Brent to just step back and pretend it was none of his business.

5

Cooper was still shaking when he reached his father's shop. What had he done? He certainly wasn't going back to school. He could barely walk, barely breathe.

"He saw me! And heard me!"

Cooper nearly screamed when Samantha suddenly reappeared. He jammed his thumb on the shop door and cussed, shaking his hand, as Samantha continued her joyous exultation.

"The guy from the library *saw* me," she said. Cooper tried to look mellow as he crossed the shop and headed toward the back room. The girl working at the counter gave him a quizzical look, but let him by. "It was only for a moment, and he was pretty out of it, but he saw me, and then he could hear me."

" 'Pretty out of it,' " Cooper grumbled, looking around

for his father. "Because of what *I* did to him. I don't even *know* what happened, but it was . . . I mean, what *was* that?"

"I don't know, but it was cool, and I think you should experiment with doing it again," Samantha answered as they both stepped into the back room.

"No!" Cooper nearly shouted, shocked that she would even suggest such a thing.

The back door opened and his father stepped inside from the employee parking lot where they kept the Dumpsters. He stopped, consulted his watch, and then gave Cooper a pointed look after confirming it was still during school hours.

"I'm not feeling well," Cooper mumbled, hoping the extent to which he was pale and trembling made the excuse believable.

His father still looked skeptical, but just said, "If you're sick, stay in the employee area and away from the food. If you start feeling better, you can come out front and give me a hand at the register."

Cooper was grateful that his father wasn't the type to probe further—yet. He would expect answers later, but would give Cooper some time to calm down first.

Cooper's mother had tried to convince him to see a shrink about a month ago when it became obvious that he wasn't sleeping, and had no interest in getting back in touch with his friends. They had ended up shouting, all of them. Cooper had never raised his voice to his parents before, and he couldn't remember the last time they had yelled.

They hadn't discussed the subject again since, but he remembered his father's view of the situation: *Sometimes we need time to heal in our own way, without doctors telling us what we should be feeling.*

"Are you okay?" Samantha finally asked as Cooper collapsed against a wall in the employees' lounge and slid down to sit on the floor.

"Just *fine.*" Sarcasm wasn't his natural tone, but sometimes Samantha brought it out of him. "What did I do back there? It was like—"

It was if a part of him over which he had no control had shoved Brent away—except that Brent's *body* had never moved, only collapsed in on itself. Afterward, Cooper felt like he was looking at a corpse.

Cooper squeezed his eyes shut, trying to block out the memory of the first time that had happened, in the hospital. He had woken up in the hospital only a few minutes before, and there had been so many doctors and nurses and people asking questions and poking and prodding him. He had just wanted them all to go *away*—

He bowed his head and drew a deep breath.

"Look, Brent was okay," Samantha said awkwardly. "I stayed until he stood up and walked out. He's all right. It's no big deal."

"No big deal," Cooper repeated. "Samantha, I see ghosts—"

"Just one."

"Fine, one ghost," he said, continuing more firmly, "and now I have another freakish thing going on."

"Technically, you've had that as long as I've known you," Samantha joked. "You've just kind of avoided people so you haven't—I'm not helping, am I?"

"Not so much," he said, and yet her awkward attempt almost brought a smile to his face.

"If you're so worried, talk to him," Samantha said. "You could look for him at the library again, or ask the librarian if she knows his last name so you can look up his phone number. Or just ask around at Q-tech on Monday."

Cooper shook his head. "I doubt he wants to talk to me. He probably doesn't want anything to do with me."

"You're such a *coward*, Cooper Blake," Samantha snapped. "You wouldn't talk to that girl earlier when it was perfectly obvious she was trying to leave you an opportunity, no questions asked. And now you meet someone who might be able to help you, might even *want* to help you, and you're running away as fast as you can. What about your *friends*? You don't call anyone, and barely talk to people in the hall, even when I hear them call your name. I know you don't talk to your parents, even when you all sit around the table together. I'm your only friend at the moment and I swear the only reason *I* talk to you is because no one else can hear me."

Cooper blinked, startled by the tirade.

"I wouldn't even know where to start with Delilah and the others," he said.

"It's not like they don't know . . . what happened," she said, sounding as unwilling as he was to remember the details out loud. "They're probably just giving you space. I'm sure they're worried—"

"They're worried, sure," Cooper interrupted. "They would be even more worried if they knew what was *actually* going on, and then instead of dealing with my issues, I would be dealing with *their* issues with my issues. I don't want to have to take care of other people, not until I'm okay taking care of myself."

"Coward," Samantha said again with a flounce of her currently neon orange, yellow and pink hair.

"I'm not a coward!" Cooper protested, before realizing he was speaking loudly, and clamping his mouth shut.

He stood up. The shaking had mostly subsided.

"Come on, just talk to Brent," Samantha said. "If not to help you, then for *me*. Unless you want to be stuck with me the rest of your natural life?"

"You're charming, but I could live without you."

"So go talk to him. He saw me for a moment, and he talked back to me. He'll believe you. It doesn't just have to be you and me trying to figure this out. Because, I hate to break it to you, but you're not very good at the whole magic and mythology stuff."

"I'm a football player," he grumbled.

"No, you're an *ex*-football player, the same way you're probably an ex-friend to at least a few people."

"The doctors told me I wouldn't be able to play, any-way," Cooper said—before opening the door to face his father up front.

"Yeah, they told you that you couldn't play football. But

not that you couldn't have a life." She shook her head and sighed. "You work, then. I'll look for him. Do reconnaissance. I'll try to get him to hear me."

Cooper could only stare as she walked off. Maybe she was right. Samantha's support was all that had gotten him through the first weeks of physical therapy, when everything hurt all the time. It had been early August before he had been able to walk across a room on his own. Samantha had been the one who kept him going and convinced him to keep trying, back when he was sure he would be a painful wreck the rest of his life.

He owed it to her to do whatever he could to help her, too.

First, though, he waited for his father to finish the order he was working on and gesture to Cooper to follow him a few paces from the register.

"Cooper . . ." He had a sinking feeling in his stomach as his father took a deep, thoughtful breath, and finally just asked, "What happened?"

Cooper hated lying to his parents, but contrary to what Brent thought, he had gotten pretty good at it. The trick was to keep it as close to the truth as possible, and to include something the other person wanted to hear.

"I was at the library, and ran into a friend," he said, meaning Brent, a slight exaggeration but one that would make his father happy. "We got to talking about what happened this summer, and it brought a lot of stuff back. I couldn't handle going back to school right away."

He knew his father assumed Cooper meant the accident, though he was actually referring to Samantha. But all in all, his words were pretty much honest.

His father nodded. "Okay, then. Thanks for telling me." He turned back to the coffee machine, as one of their regulars came in. By the time his father had prepared her order, he had come to a decision. "Cooper, get an apron on and watch the register for me. I'll let the school know I forgot to call them before taking you out for a doctor's appointment this afternoon."

Cooper breathed a sigh of relief as he did as instructed.

Before leaving the front room, however, his father added, "I'm covering for you this *once,* by the way, because you're seventeen, you've always been a responsible young man, and I believe you're doing what you need to do. But if I start hearing from the school that you're skipping classes or not getting your work done on a regular basis, we're going to have a longer talk. Understand?"

Cooper nodded. "I understand."

If today was any indication of how the school year was going to go, then he suspected the next "talk" was going to come sooner rather than later—and it was going to be the least of his problems.

Cooper could barely keep his eyes open after dinner. True to his word, his father hadn't mentioned his brief sojourn from class to his mother, and their awkward chatter barely masked the conversations his parents obviously wanted to have with him, but couldn't. The effort exhausted Cooper, and he crawled into bed without taking off anything more than his shoes, too tired to even experience the anxiety that usually accompanied the descent into sleep.

The instant the rain began, he knew bad things were coming. It started with patchy clouds, barely wispy, but as he continued driving down the endless highway they darkened and spread. Soon a fine mist was falling, but if anything, it seemed like the weather had improved visibility, since before the cloud cover built, the afternoon sun's glare had been blinding.

But he knew better.

He couldn't remember the details of what happened next, but he re-membered the emotions and the physical sensations. He struggled against them. He knew he was dreaming, and he pulled his car over to the side of the highway and got out—

As soon as his feet touched the pavement, he was back in the car.

This time he just took his foot off the gas, and let the car coast to a stop—

Then it was back to seventy miles an hour, and the brakes didn't work anymore, and the car wouldn't slow down.

Black tendrils began to rise from the pavement, waiting for him. The highway went on forever without a single exit, and tall concrete barriers rose into the darkening sky on each side.

Cooper screamed with frustration, put one hand on the wheel, and spun it as fast as he could to the side.

The car began to spin like a top, incredibly fast for impossibly long.

Cooper shot upright, a scream trapped in the back of his throat. People had told him the gist of what had happened in his accident, and he was grateful he couldn't recall the rest.

Except in his nightmares.

He shuddered and stood, eliciting a sharp pain in his hip. He should have stretched before falling asleep.

He took a warm shower, hoping the pounding water would dull the ache that ran up his side from his knee almost to his shoulder. It was ten at night, and his parents were sleeping like the dead—

Wrong simile.

The sound of running water wouldn't wake them, anyway.

After his shower, he stopped in front of the full-length mirror attached to the inside of the bathroom door. With a towel around his waist, he examined his physique with a critical eye.

He had never been *big*, compared to most football players, but he had certainly lost muscle mass since the accident.

During the day, his long sleeves covered the scars that crisscrossed up and down his arms. Some of them were starting to fade to shiny pink-white, but many were still darker, revealing the depth of the initial wounds. Those same sleeves covered the ragged patch on his shoulder, now mottled pink and brown, where most of the skin had been ripped off by the hot pavement; his pants normally hid similar marks on his left hip and knee. The clothes also hid the surgery scars, and the faint—almost gone, or was the color entirely in his head, these days?—bruises that lingered on his ribs.

Clothes, those simple defenses, hid all evidence of the accident from sight. They made him appear whole. Now if only his mind could agree. During the day he could barely remember anything, but during the night the floodgates opened. If he closed his eyes, he would see...hear... smell...taste...

"So vain," Samantha teased as she walked through the wall.

"Ever hear of *privacy*?" he snapped as he checked that his

towel was snugly in place. The words were sharp, but he was pretty well resigned to the fact that Samantha didn't care about his privacy or anyone else's.

"Don't remember," she replied glibly. "Maybe I heard of it and just forgot."

"Well, would you leave so I can put on some clothes?"

"Don't be a prude. They say you used to be a football star. You must have changed in plenty of locker rooms."

"Yeah. With *guys*," he answered. "You're not a guy."

"I'm hardly a girl, either," she argued. "I'm *dead*."

"Fine. Dead. Whatever. So why do you want to stay?"

"Because you're sexy-cute," she replied promptly.

"Out!"

She sighed, and wandered back through the wall, mumbling, "Sometimes I wish I was the *invisible* kind of ghost."

Cooper shook his head. Why couldn't he have gotten a *guy* kind of ghost? The kind of ghost who would certainly never show up while he was in the shower or encourage him to track down and be friendly with guys from Q-tech.

As soon as he had pulled on his pajama pants, Samantha appeared again. Cooper had a sneaking suspicion she had been watching, but didn't want that confirmed and wouldn't trust her if she denied it, so he didn't bring it up.

She sat on the bed beside him, one leg tucked beneath her, and one dangling through the piece of furniture. He wondered what kind of effort or thought it took to keep her from falling through floors or furniture more than she chose to.

"I found Brent," she said, "but no luck there. He was passed out with a pillow over his head."

"We'll find his number and call him as soon as school is out tomorrow," Cooper promised. He didn't want to do it, but he owed it to her.

Samantha smiled, but her expression seemed half-hearted. "I hate nighttime," she confided. "Everyone going about, sleeping, dreaming or snuggling with other people or partying or *something*. And then there's just me."

"Trade?" Cooper proposed. He would have been happy to stay up alone, if it meant he didn't have those dreams Samantha envied.

Samantha lay back. Cooper was about to yell at her about the whole "girl" thing again, but she wasn't flirting this time. Instead, she took a funeral pose, with her arms crossed neatly across her chest. She closed her eyes and sighed.

"To sleep, perchance to dream and stuff," she misquoted softly. "I'm really bored, Cooper. I'm getting kind of desperate."

Without thinking about it, he reached out to awkwardly pat her shoulder. He realized what he was doing and pulled back before actually touching her, but her eyes had cracked open, and she half smiled.

"I'm going to go wander," she said. "Look in windows. Or something."

She sank through the bed and out of sight.

Cooper was almost certain Samantha had actually left this time, but still, he found himself staring at the spot where she had just been—his bed, which he had come to see as a kind of enemy, one he seemed to battle nightly.

Sometimes sleep didn't come at all. He would spend hours lying there, fighting to keep his eyes closed and his body relaxed, but every time he started to slip into sleep, it was like he could *feel* the nightmares reaching for him. If he cracked his eyes open in that state, he saw shadows that didn't match any light source. They lingered around him and even more thickly around Samantha, and upon seeing them he would jerk back awake with a start.

Instead of going back to bed now, he took some time to try to read the assignment for English, but couldn't absorb most of the words. Lately his memory was simply *shot*. He did a couple of math problems and read three or four paragraphs of his history textbook, and then chucked the book across the room—only to cringe as it narrowly missed the window. He didn't want to explain shattered glass to his parents.

He booted up the computer, and lost himself in Wikipedia for a while, then spent a good half hour looking at cat macros before he broke down and logged into his MMORPG pirates game. He couldn't quite resist opening the one e-mail in his account, which was from Delilah, but all it said was, *If you're in trouble, Cooper, you can talk to me. I might be more understanding than you would expect.*

By then, however, it was one in the morning and his eyelids were so heavy they seemed to be dragging his head down. His eyes kept unfocusing so he had to roll away from the computer, and the dizziness of exhaustion made him lie down. Ignoring the blankets, he collapsed onto the bed.

The first time he jerked back from sleep, his heart was pounding and there was a sour taste in his mouth. 1:45. He pulled a pillow over his head. He only had a couple of hours left until his alarm was due to go off. He couldn't possibly dream on only a couple of hours' sleep.

7

Cooper Blake was in trouble. Delilah hadn't decided yet what she planned to do about that, if anything, but it had taken only a moment for her to know that Cooper was in way over his head and sinking fast. It was now the middle of the night . . . no, well *past* the middle of the night . . . and her mind was still on the problem.

Unlike most members and supporters of the Lenmark Ocelots' football team, Delilah had not gone to visit Cooper in the hospital. She knew about the accident, of course, but though she had many interesting skills, she was no doctor; there would have been no point in her loitering by his side while he was comatose.

She knew Cooper had been unconscious for three days. She couldn't help hearing about it from the other girls on the squad, the guys on the team, her friends on the school paper, and everyone else she ran in to, all of whom it seemed wanted to offer emotional support, or ask for it.

It wasn't that she didn't like Cooper; he was hard to dislike. He was the kind of person who, when presented with the opportunity to do a good deed, didn't have the sense to contemplate being selfish instead. A total sweetheart, which meant he wasn't interesting enough to be her type for dating, but he was fun to keep around as a friend. Indeed, she would've been sad if he had died . . . but he was still alive and kicking, so she didn't know why everyone had made such a big deal about it.

What that meant, though, was that she hadn't sought Cooper out in the hospital or at school since his return, and so had no idea how long he had looked this bad. People normally didn't get that coated in psychic filth without dabbling in heavy magics. But unless Delilah had seriously misjudged him somewhere along the way, Cooper was no amateur sorcerer. She had to look for another source.

If Delilah hadn't known what Cooper was normally like, she wouldn't have felt driven to help him. After all, he wasn't on the team anymore, he hadn't called her, and he had snubbed her attempt to be nice. Under any other circumstance, she would have said that if he wanted to huddle in his own mystic mishap, that was his prerogative. However, Cooper was so infested with dark power, he probably couldn't help being jittery, couldn't help seeking isolation. He would draw back from those he was close to instinctively, even if he didn't consciously realize his infection was a danger to those around him.

Delilah sat cross-legged on her down comforter and shut her eyes now, centering her awareness.

She knew from experience that there were beasts in the shadows of the world; they had nearly killed her when she was twelve. They scurried about intent on nothing more than sating their own hunger. They latched on to the weak to feed, bloating themselves until their hosts somehow shook free of them, or died from the infection.

Sure enough, when Delilah opened her eyes, her attention focused not on the physical world but the paranormal one instead, she saw the hungry shadows pacing around her. Ryan le Coire had told her that those few individuals who could see these beasts all perceived them differently; they always reminded Delilah of some kind of centipede or other vile, multi-legged creature, slithering and grasping at everything they touched. They must have caught her scent when she stopped to talk to Cooper.

The sight of them made her skin crawl. She crossed her arms across her chest and fought the instinct to run. Running would give them an opening.

She walked slowly to the window, which she opened fully. The fresh night air would help her focus. She wasn't strong enough to banish the shadows completely, but if she was careful, she could keep them from making a meal out of her. Eventually they would tire of stalking prey they had no hope of taking down.

It would have been a wild coincidence if Cooper's current state was not related to the accident, so Delilah opened her laptop, signed on to the neighbors' unsecured wireless network—their own fault for not bothering to set a password—and looked up the event she had only barely paid attention to at the time.

She skimmed headlines as they came up.

MAJOR ACCIDENT ON INTERSTATE KILLS TWO, LEAVES FOUR IN CRITICAL CONDITION.

WET ROADS BLAMED FOR EIGHT-CAR PILEUP ON I-90.

She read article after article, starting with national press and then focusing on local news outlets, which had given more attention to Cooper instead of chattering endlessly about the celebrity involved in the crash.

From what she could put together, a patch of fog had turned slightly slippery roads into a zero-visibility death trap. One witness said she thought she saw a deer or some other animal in her rearview mirror. She had passed safely out of the fog, but the driver of the car behind her had slammed on the brakes, and because the drivers of the cars behind it weren't able to see what was happening, disaster had followed.

Delilah had already known that Cooper's survival had been questionable when he had first been rushed to the hospital. The doctors who performed the emergency surgeries required to save his life were quoted in the paper, calling Cooper's recovery "miraculous."

A little more research revealed that Cooper had been

driving the car in front. After he had hit the brakes, his car had spun out, and he had been thrown through the windshield and onto the pavement at seventy miles per hour. One article reported that he may have been hit by another vehicle after that.

He should have been dead. No wonder the shadows were following him. They had hooked their claws into him, ready to feast on the remnants of his mortality once he gave up, but then he had denied them. He had lived.

And he *still* lived.

That meant the papers had gotten the story wrong. This was not just a jock who survived a car accident. Something more powerful than a mere human being had claimed Cooper and kept him alive. For Cooper's benefit? Maybe, but unlikely, judging by Cooper's lack of experience with the occult.

Most people were lucky enough to never know the scavengers existed. Healthy individuals could usually break free of their grasp without even realizing they had been bitten, like fighting off the common cold. Even Brent, Ryan's golden-boy telepath, was completely blind to them, since he had never bothered to expand his powers beyond his inborn knack for reading minds.

Those who worked with greater magics, however, and struggled to make more of themselves the way Delilah did, attracted the shadows' attention. They had scared her so much the first time she saw them when she was twelve that she had backed off and refused to do so much as touch a

Ouija board—until Ryan le Coire picked her out of a crowd during a freshman field trip into the city, and told her she had a great deal of latent power, which he could teach her how to use.

She believed in meeting one's potential.

So even though it was already two in the morning, Delilah set her alarm for five. There were rituals she needed to perform in the morning, to strengthen her shields before the school day began, to make sure none of Cooper's shadows could set its teeth into her.

As soon as school was out, Delilah would confer with her associates, and then she would have plenty to say when she spoke to Cooper again.

Brent was in a full sweat. He had suddenly remembered that he wasn't enrolled in Q-tech, but had changed to the public school. He had missed the entire first week of classes!

He scrambled to gather school supplies, but his mother had sent his backpack to his grandmother in Japan to repair a broken strap, and he didn't own a single pen, pencil, or notebook.

The last time he was in the public high school building was for pre-freshman orientation, and he had no idea where his classes were or even what he was signed up for. He found the main office finally, and they gave him a schedule, but his first class was all the way on the eighty-fifth floor and the elevator was out of order. By the time he got there, class was over, and he had to go downstairs again.

The second class was studying relativistic physics. After making an apple explode by dipping it in nitroglycerin and throwing it at the window, the teacher distributed the first exam, worth thirty percent of his final grade.

He couldn't even read the test. It had only been a week! How could they already be talking about these things?

He stood up, and only when people started laughing did he realize he was completely naked.

"Oo, cute," a girl said.

He turned, blushing, and the dream—for, upon standing nude in front of the class, he had gratefully realized it had to be a dream—shifted. The classroom and his classmates disappeared, replaced by a white room full of streaks of lights and sharp, clanging sounds. There were windows of various shapes and sizes around the room, and all he could see beyond them was pouring rain. Many of the windows were open, so rain cascaded down their sills and water pooled beneath them, seemingly as deep as a lake.

And of course there was the girl, her long blond hair clipped back with oversize hairpins with pink rhinestones. She was wearing a black tank top and a green skirt over black and blue striped stockings. She sat perched upon a white stool in the middle of one of those swirling pools, while dark shadowy figures reached for her.

The figures gave Brent a chill, but he made himself look away from them. This was just a dream, after all; he wouldn't let it become a nightmare. Instead, he looked down, focused, and brought pants and a T-shirt into the dream.

More suitably dressed, he asked the girl, "Are you here to lend me a pencil?"

She tilted her head, looking curious. "You know you're dreaming?" she asked.

"I lucid dream a lot these days," he answered.

"Do you see ghosts a lot, too?"

He straightened up, now intrigued. "Are you Cooper's ghost?"

She frowned. "*His?* I'm not a new kitten or something. I'm just . . . me. Samantha. It's totally not my decision that he's the only person who can see me. But you saw me for a little while, too. How did you do that?"

"How did Cooper do whatever *he* did to me?"

"There isn't time to explain everything," she said, shaking her head. "And I don't know the answer to that one anyway. But you've got to come see us. Can you help him?"

"I was going to call," he lied, unable to admit to her that he had kind of planned to foist the entire problem off on Ryan without ever getting personally involved.

"You can come by the coffee shop! The one in the center of town. Cooper works there every morning before school, starting at four-thirty, and then on the weekends until noon. He's shy, but I'll make him talk to you. And let you in if the shop isn't open yet."

"I don't actually know a lot about *real* ghosts," Brent admitted. "I know a lot of stories and legends, but none that are like the way he described you." Wondering if he might have better luck with Samantha than with Cooper, he asked, "Do you know what happened that triggered his being able to see you?"

She paused, chewing on her lower lip.

"There was an accident," she answered. "He doesn't talk about it. But he was in the hospital a long time. I only harassed him about it because I thought maybe . . . you know . . . it would be relevant to me? But we looked into it. It wasn't how we . . . you know . . . *met*."

"Accident?" Brent asked. "Like a car accident, or something weirder?"

"Car," she responded tersely. "It freaks him out to think about it. And he's the only one I've got, really, so I don't like to think about it, either." He was just thinking that he could probably look it up in the local paper when she added, "Please don't tell him I told you. And don't tell anyone else."

"Even if it means I can help him, or you?"

"Do you really think you *can* help?" she asked. She stopped again, looking pensive. "Even if you don't know about real ghosts, maybe you could help with research? Books aren't Cooper's strong suit."

"I can probably do more than that," Brent answered. "I kind of have an unusual ability. There's a guy who taught me how to use that ability without it hurting me. He's the one who taught me how to lucid dream, for instance, since I need to be able to do so in order to keep out of other people's heads while I sleep. He might be able to—"

This time, Brent knew he was awake, as he slammed the snooze button on his alarm clock before realizing the offensive sound was coming from his neighbor's car alarm instead. His clock and a pile of books tumbled to the floor.

"Sorry," he said out loud, in case Samantha was still there, listening.

He lay back down, but sleep eluded him. It was only 3:47 in the morning, but now that he was awake, the images from his dream felt more threatening, not less. He remembered the worst part of Cooper pushing him in the library—not the sensation of losing control over his body, of maybe even losing his flesh entirely, but the sight of the hungry darkness that had come for him during the instant he had been in that helpless state.

If Cooper's ghost was real, then those *things* were real, too.

The dark, which hadn't frightened him since he had been a little kid, suddenly seemed menacing, and it wasn't until he stood up and turned on the light that he could get his heart to stop pounding.

He leaned back against the wall, trying to feel under control. He could hear it in his ears, the beat of his heart and the swish of frantically flowing blood. He bowed his head, dizzy, and then lifted it again as he heard someone say, *Damn neighbors. That car makes a ruckus every night. Someone should do something—*

No, that wasn't out loud; that was someone across the street, thinking angry thoughts as he tossed in bed.

I am so dead. The first night they let me take the car and now it's hours after curfew. Maybe I can tell them I had to be the designated—

—never going to let her take the car again. Grounded for the rest of her—

—maybe I should just call. I don't even care if I wake him up. I should break this off now, before—

—nothing rhymes with that. I'm never going to finish this—

Brent collapsed to his knees, squeezed his eyes shut, and pressed his hands to his temples as if warding off a headache. He struggled to pull his mind inward, and push everyone else *out*.

He could do this. He had spent months with Ryan learning how to do this. He just needed to focus.

What is all that noise? Banging at all times of night and day.

He struggled to his feet as he picked up on his mother's waspish thoughts. The combination of the clock falling and his knees hitting the floor must have woken her. If he was lucky, her sleeping pills still had enough of a grip on her that she would roll over and fall back asleep, but Brent had learned better than to trust his fate to luck.

He made it to his bedroom door, which he locked before

grabbing clothes and almost falling through the first-story window and out of their tiny house. Woods. He wanted to be away from people for a little while. Mum could pound on the door and cuss at an empty room for as long as she liked.

He fought back the onslaught of strangers' and friends' thoughts long enough to make it under the cool canopy of the forest.

As he finally managed to breathe again, he looked up and realized he had come to the same spot where he had first met Delilah last fall. He had stayed away since they had broken up in March, partially in an attempt to avoid her, and partially because he hadn't needed to come to the forest since she had introduced him to Ryan. It was a nice spot. Quiet. It was Delilah's private ritual space, and she had wrapped it in magics that blocked out other, invasive powers. She hadn't specifically warded it for telepathy, a power she lacked, but it helped a little, anyway. Now, it also kept the voices that tormented him at bay, and allowed him to clear his head.

It was probably also designed to keep out the shadowy forms he had seen in the library and in his room. Delilah hadn't talked to him much about the dangers witches faced when they did magic, but he knew there were things she was afraid of in the dark, no matter how much she tried to pretend otherwise.

It was time to leave. Delilah came here enough nights that he was risking a run-in.

Maybe he *should* try to catch Cooper, as the ghost had suggested. He could always go back to sleep later, after the other kids were at school, and his mother had given up on him and gone back to bed. After the sun was up, when he could stand to close his eyes.

Cooper had managed to avoid dreaming again, but that mostly just meant he hadn't slept long enough to get to that stage of sleep, which meant he hadn't slept long enough, *period*. The third time his father caught him staring into space at the espresso machine, he had been told to go to the front and set up, and leave anything hot, sharp or complicated alone.

He jumped at the sudden banging now, only to realize that it was just someone knocking on the door. He glanced at the clock—still half an hour until they opened—and called, "We're closed!"

When the next round of knocking started, Cooper dropped coffee grounds all over the counter. At least he had just rewashed that counter for the day, and dried it, so he could sweep the grounds into a filter instead of having to throw them all out.

"Oh, for the love of . . . ," he grumbled as the knocking grew louder. He was now in sight of the door, so he looked up with a disgruntled glare.

Oh. *Him.* They made eye contact, and Brent gave a self-conscious wave before shoving his hands in his pockets.

"Who's pounding on the door?" Cooper's father called.

"Someone I know, apparently," Cooper answered. "Sorry. I have no idea what he wants. Mind if I let him in?"

"A friend?" he asked.

"I guess," Cooper replied. Brent hadn't run screaming, at least, and Cooper *had* promised Samantha he would try to look him up. . . .

"If he's a friend, open the door and get him a cup of coffee," his father said a little too jovially.

Cooper unlocked the door with a strange, fatalistic feeling. For a few moments, he and Brent stood there, looking at each other, neither sure what to say.

Cooper noticed that Brent kept a good distance, and did *not* offer to shake hands. That was fine. Cooper wasn't anxious to risk tossing him across the room again, anyway.

Awkwardly, Brent said, "Your friend told me I could find you here."

"What friend?" Cooper grumbled. Some of the guys from the team knew where he was, but he had trouble picturing them talking to Brent about Cooper. Or about anything.

Very quietly, Brent said, "I think she was probably your . . . you know." He glanced past Cooper, where his father was standing in the doorway with flour on his hands, obviously wanting to make sure Cooper invited Brent in instead of telling him to go away.

"Come inside," Cooper said as goose bumps ran up his arms. It was one thing for Brent to enthusiastically make up fantastic stories in the library, as if for his own amusement; it was another to find him here, subdued, serious, and seeming to truly believe Cooper's tale. "I've got to finish setting up the front, but I can get you a coffee or something."

"Thanks."

As Brent stepped through the doorway, Cooper said, "Her name is Samantha, by the way." Saying it, admitting out loud that she existed to another person, seemed like it lifted a weight off his shoulders.

"Yeah, she mentioned," Brent repeated. "She's . . . interesting, isn't she?"

His father had finally ducked back into the next room, at which point Cooper relaxed some. "Yeah. Kind of painful sense of color."

"We're definitely talking about the same girl," Brent agreed, good humor in his voice now despite the rings of exhaustion under his eyes. "But she seems to care about you."

"She's nice," Cooper said. "Not big on privacy, but I think mostly it's that she's lonely. I'm surprised she isn't here yet, actually. She normally chats all through the morning."

"Huh," Brent answered. Then he blinked and shook his whole body. "Sorry. Did you say something about coffee? I'm not used to being awake at this hour."

"Sit down. I'll get you a cup. How do you take it?"

"Just . . . coffeelike. Black. I'm a Dunkin' Donuts guy," Brent said by way of explanation. "Complicated coffee confuses me."

Cooper's father emerged from the back as Cooper poured Brent a cup of their house roast. "If you want to hang out with your friend, I have things under control," he said.

"Thanks."

"You've been a bit of a menace this morning, anyway," he pointed out with a chuckle.

Cooper agreed and led Brent to a table in the corner, as far away from the counter—and his father—as they could get.

"So," Cooper began, once they were seated across from each other.

"So," Brent replied. "Since I've seen her, too, I'm going to work on the assumption that you're not crazy. I think that's a good place to start."

Cooper nodded. "You're responding to all this a lot better than I did at first."

"My life's been pretty weird for a while now," Brent explained. "I'll tell you all about it when we get to that. What else can you tell me about Samantha and . . . um, yourself?"

Cooper wondered if Brent had almost asked something else, but he decided it didn't matter.

"You said you saw her?" Cooper asked, curious. "No one else has been able to see her before now."

"I don't think I normally can," Brent said, "but right after whatever you did in the library—and we'll get to *that*, too—I saw and heard her for a second or two. Last night I saw her when I was dreaming."

Dreaming? Dear God, it was bad enough when she showed up while he was getting dressed or something. If that girl showed up in Cooper's dreams—

"Calm," Brent said softly. "Wherever you're going right now, it's not a good place to go."

Cooper's eyes widened as he focused back on Brent, and *not* on the nightmares. "What are you, some kind of shrink?" he snapped.

"Not . . . exactly," Brent said, his voice smooth and careful. "But I know your mind goes somewhere bad sometimes. It's somewhere you don't like to think about. It *hurts*. My guess is it has something to do with Samantha and your ability to see her. But I'm better with computers than with human brains, so I'm not going to try to figure out what the issue is with yours. What I can do is recommend a witch I know."

"A . . . *witch?*" Cooper repeated. First ghosts, now witches. Why couldn't this get less weird instead of more?

"Call him a witch, a sorcerer, a psychic, whatever makes you comfortable," Brent answered. "The point is, he knows more about this supernatural stuff than anyone I've ever met. He helped me, and I'm sure he can help you."

"What did he do for you?" Cooper asked. If Brent hadn't mentioned that he had seen Samantha, Cooper probably would have brushed him off as a quack already.

Of course, Brent hadn't exactly *described* Samantha. And Cooper had been the one to volunteer her name.

He didn't want to be cynical. He *really* didn't want to be cynical, because he desperately needed to be able to talk to someone about all this. But until Samantha showed up to confirm she had spoken to Brent in a dream the night before, Cooper couldn't help remaining a little suspicious.

"Well . . ." Brent hesitated, staring at his coffee. "I was hearing voices. Which turned out to be thoughts. At first I figured I was going crazy, but people kept saying or doing things I had just heard them think. It got so bad that I couldn't hide that I was having problems. Starting at Q-tech helped, since I could focus on more hands-on projects instead of just sitting in a classroom all day, but by sophomore year it got to be too much. I collapsed at school, and they sent me to the emergency room. I spent the next couple of months going to doctor after doctor as they did a million tests. I wasn't about to tell them I was hearing voices, so eventually they prescribed me medication for migraines, which didn't work, of course. I spent summer vacation checking out psychics, anyone in the area who said they had power. Most of them are complete charlatans, but last fall I met someone who passed my name on to Ryan. He walked up to me as I was in the middle of dismantling a hard drive and just asked me outright, 'What am I thinking?' "

"And?" Cooper prompted as Brent took a slow sip of his coffee.

"And I was sick of all the BS I had gone through recently, so I looked. I *really* tried, and I got nothing. With most people, when I look at them, I get babble. Very few people have just one solid thought at a time. I get a lot of background static when I try to read you, though; you have a lot of thoughts you've got shoved away, and that makes the rest of your thoughts very focused, which is a nice change. But trying to read Ryan was like looking at a blank wall: you can tell it's there, but that's about it."

The bit about reading Cooper's thoughts was a little creepy. When Brent had made a comment earlier about Cooper's mind going somewhere bad, telepathy hadn't jumped at him as the most likely explanation. Now he was glad he didn't have anything to hide except for the haunting Brent already knew about.

"And he didn't decide you were a fake right then and there because you couldn't answer him?" Cooper asked.

"I looked at him and he stood there completely calm as I got more and more frustrated," Brent answered. "Finally, I told him the truth, that I couldn't hear a damn thing. He smiled, and sat down next to me and said he had heard that I was looking for someone to help me learn to control my ability. Then suddenly I heard his voice in my head, as clear as day, saying, 'I can help you.' I couldn't read him because he's used to spending time with people who can, so he knows how to shield himself. If I'd been a fake, or crazy, I would've bluffed and come up with something. When I admitted I couldn't hear anything, he knew I had to be for real."

"That's pretty intense," Cooper said, despite still feeling that wriggle of doubt. "And you think he knows about ghosts?"

Brent hesitated, long enough to make Cooper nervous.

"I don't know what he knows," Brent answered after a minute. "Ryan and I and—well, we got into a conversation about the afterlife once. Ryan doesn't bother meditating on God or religion, and I know he doesn't believe in ghosts as solid personalities the way you describe Samantha, or even the way they show up in stories. He says sometimes the dead leave behind imprints on places or things, but those are just remnants of power in the form of emotion or single, key memories or impulses. I don't know what he'll make of Samantha."

So the miracle witch—or whatever—might not know a thing.

Cooper's disappointment must have shown on his face because Brent added, "That doesn't mean he'll be useless. Ryan's kind of like a scientist. He won't discount what's right in front of his face just because of his previous beliefs. If there's one thing he taught me—beyond how to control my own ability—it's that this world is full of more weird

things than we can imagine. Samantha might be something he's never seen before, but that doesn't mean he
won't be helpful."

Cooper was still skeptical. "Would it piss you off if I
asked you what I'm thinking?" To make it fair, he tried to
focus on something particular. The number forty-two;
that would work. Forty-two.

Brent shook his head. "You don't want me to answer
that."

"Sure I do, or I wouldn't have asked," Cooper insisted,
his doubts increasing as Brent stalled.

"Seriously, you *don't*. You don't realize how many thoughts
cross your mind in a single second."

"Seriously, I *do*."

Brent shut his eyes and said flatly, "Forty-two. And cars.
Rain. Noise. Where's Samantha? The cars again. Now the
image in the mirror. Scars. Samantha again. Your father's
glad you're talking to a friend—he's actually humming in
the back room, something from *Fiddler on the Roof,* which he
saw with you years ago. For your eighth birthday. You
had strawberry cake with chocolate frosting. It was a
Colt Hatchback . . . 2003. Green . . . blue. Greenish blue.
You argued with your mom over what color the car was.
Rain, and—"

"Stop it!"

Brent opened his eyes. "I won't do it again," he promised. "Calm."

"Don't you *tell* me to be—"

"Cool it!" Brent shouted. At least, it seemed like a shout. Cooper didn't think Brent had actually raised his voice, but the word echoed in Cooper's mind. "I didn't do this to you. Someday you're going to have to square with those memories, those thoughts. For now, though, I just needed you to believe me. Do you believe me?"

"I believe you."

He certainly didn't want another demonstration.

10

Brent waited, sipping his coffee, until Cooper's agitation had subsided. The coffee was bitter, stronger than he was used to, but it was palatable enough and it gave him something else to focus on so Cooper didn't feel even more on the spot.

He didn't have to make an effort to read Cooper. In fact, even when he made an effort *not* to, Cooper's clear, surface thoughts were sometimes hard to tune out.

"I assume you have to go to school today?" he asked, once Cooper's thoughts had settled back into something manageable.

Cooper nodded. "I skipped yesterday afternoon. I don't intend to make a habit of it."

"I could grab you from school after classes are over, and drive us to—" Brent winced as his words elicited a series of pain-filled images from Cooper. "Or we could take the train into the city. We can get to Ryan's via public transportation."

"You said you weren't going to read my mind again," Cooper said, but there was a halfhearted quality to his objection.

"I won't try to read you intentionally unless I have to, and I'll try not to prod you with anything I hear, but when you shove thoughts at me like iron pokers through my eyes, I'm going to respond," Brent said bluntly.

"Like . . . iron . . . *pokers*? Didn't you say you mostly got static?"

"Mostly, yes, but that's the background. Your thoughts in front can be pretty sharp," Brent said, reminding himself to watch his words. He had to admit, he had never thought he would be having this particular conversation with the regular-high's football star, but weirder things had happened. He had stopped believing jock stereotypes after seeing Delilah practice magic in the middle of the woods, and learning a week later that she was also the captain of the cheerleading squad. "Mostly I can control things now," he added, still trying to convince Cooper to come with him and get help. "It was a lot worse before."

"Hmm." Cooper paused, his gaze going distant. Then he glanced up at Brent, searchingly. He seemed about to speak, then stopped again, and finally said, "It's really weird talking to someone who can read my mind."

"Trust me, it's just as weird from the other side," Brent

answered honestly. "If it makes you feel better, most of the time, I really don't *want* to hear anyone's thoughts. You'd be amazed how many random and really unpleasant things cross people's minds. You know how sometimes you'll get a visual image of something gross or just seriously twisted? That's the kind of thing I used to pick up from people all the time—mental images I *never* wanted, because no one wants them. Like the stuff that comes to mind when someone says, 'I saw your mom buying handcuffs yesterday.' "

Cooper's expression at that moment was priceless.

"Okay," he said. "I could get why you wouldn't want to see that kind of stuff."

Brent waited patiently for Cooper to decide what he wanted to do.

At last, Cooper broke the silence by saying, "Tomorrow. I can't skip school again, but tomorrow would be good."

Saturday. Brent's last free weekend before school started. There was some kind of fund-raiser for the football team, so at least Delilah probably wouldn't be hanging around Ryan's when they got there. As far as he knew, Delilah and Ryan had been on rocky terms ever since the mishap that had also ended her relationship with Brent.

"Sure. Tomorrow's probably better, in terms of timing. Will you be able to get off work?"

"Yeah, no problem," Cooper said without hesitation. "I might have to cover the early morning and opening, but I doubt this Ryan guy would want us to show up at dawn anyway."

"I have to check the train schedule, but I think there's a nine-something. I'll meet you here around eight?" Brent asked.

Cooper nodded and glanced over his shoulder at the clock on the far wall. "I should get going," he said. "We need to open, and then I've got to get to school. But I'll see you tomorrow."

"Sure, sounds good," Brent said.

He drove home with every intention of looking at the public police reports, and scanning for any headlines about missing teens, accidents or abductions, but the conversation with Cooper had started a pounding in his head. It wasn't *only* for Cooper's sake that Brent hoped Ryan could help him.

His mother had passed out, thankfully, so Brent didn't need to deal with whatever inflated accusation she would come up with about where he had been. Instead, he crept back upstairs, turned out all the lights, drew the curtains, and crawled under the covers on his bed. In absolute darkness, he closed his eyes. At least the migraine had shut down his mind enough to keep the shadows at bay.

He was driving through a fine drizzle. The weather was otherwise warm and visibility wasn't too bad, so he wasn't uncomfortable. He was driving reasonably. He had his headlights on, and used his blinkers whenever he had to change lanes.

In fact, he had just put on his right signal, and looked over his shoulder to check his blind spot, when it happened.

A flash of color in front of him, almost a blur.

83

The blare of horns, screaming of brakes, screech of metal against metal—

Brent woke with a silent scream choking his throat.

Oh, *hell*. It wasn't bad enough that he was hearing thoughts and apparently dreaming ghosts—now he was sharing Cooper's post-traumatic flashback nightmares. Spending too much time with that guy was going to end up giving *Brent* a severe case of anxiety.

With any luck, he could hand Cooper over to Ryan, and Ryan would have an easy answer.

In the meantime, he went downstairs and booted up the family computer, which he had built himself and which his mother had taken possession of so she could order prescriptions without looking a pharmacist in the eye. There had to be *something* online about this girl. Then again, the search could be a little more complicated than Cooper made it out to be.

Cooper had said Samantha sounded local, but it was more true to say that she didn't seem to have any distinctive regional accent at all, at least in the short period when Brent had spoken to her. That meant she could be from anywhere in New England, the Midwest, or Northwest, at the least. She *didn't* sound southern, and she definitely sounded born-and-raised American . . . but that wasn't a lot to go on.

Searching for deaths in the area in the last few months, of course, instantly pulled up articles about Cooper's accident.

Brent swore out loud as he read the details. He had spent most of the summer at Ryan's or in the library, not watching television, and pointedly avoiding anyone from the regular high school in order to keep out of Delilah's way. He vaguely recalled Elise mentioning something about an accident one day while he had been helping her stack books, but he'd had no idea the extent of the damage.

Samantha had to be related to the accident. If she had died as a direct result of the crash, even Cooper would have made that connection, but maybe she was a family member of someone involved? Hell, for all he knew she was a guilty brake mechanic, who blamed herself for the way Cooper's car handled in the accident. The only thing he was *sure* of was that it would be too much of a coincidence if Cooper's ghost wasn't somehow connected to Cooper's near-death experience.

Well, there was one thing more to do.

He picked up the phone, and called the le Coire estate.

"Hello?" Brent wasn't surprised to hear a stranger's voice. So many people went to Ryan, either to work with him or to learn from him, that Ryan rarely bothered to answer his own phone.

"Hi," he replied. He was pretty sure he was talking to a secretary, but for all he knew he could be talking to some kind of super-mystic. "This is Brent Maresh."

"I remember you," the voice on the other end said. "Everything all right?"

"For me, yes," Brent answered. "But I have a friend who has been having some weird things happen to him, which I think Ryan might be able to help with. Or at least might be interested in. Could I talk to him, and see if he would mind if we came by?"

"I think he's working with someone right now, but I can pass on a message. When were you thinking of coming over?"

"Tomorrow morning, if that's all right."

"Mmm. Probably. What's the guy's name?"

"Cooper Blake," Brent replied, though he doubted that detail would matter to Ryan. He wasn't the type to bias his judgment of someone's power by doing much background research.

"I'll let le Coire know."

The line went dead before Brent could say good-bye.

What next?

He could call some friends and make plans, but he didn't feel the urge. He didn't have a lot of close friends these days; he had pushed most of them away in his search for some peace and silence before his hospitalization, and hadn't dared make many new ones since. If he hadn't met Delilah in such intriguing circumstances, he probably wouldn't have even let her into his life.

He grabbed his keys, and had just reached his car when the dream from earlier came washing back. He stayed there, one hand on the driver's-side door handle, until the memories had peaked and fallen, and then he forced himself to get into the car. He refused to be stuck with Cooper's issues.

It took more willpower than it should have to turn the car on, and take it out of the driveway, but by the time he reached the town center it was like his body had remembered that the accident hadn't actually happened to him. The fear and phantasmal pain faded.

To test his recovery, he merged onto the highway, and was gratified to learn that his body didn't panic. He still drove carefully—Cooper's memories remained, and would probably be vivid for a while—but he had successfully sloughed off the imprint of terror that he had picked up from Cooper.

≍11≍

Cooper just barely made it through the school day. He found his way home and ate dinner, then faced his room again.

He hadn't seen Samantha in almost twenty-four hours. In the entire time he had known her, she had never been gone so long.

Might she be *gone,* for real? If this was over, he didn't need Brent's help . . . but then what? Should he try to go back to his friends and pretend she had never existed?

He wasn't sure he could handle never knowing who she had been. Didn't he owe it to her to learn that? People shouldn't just be able to disappear without anyone noticing.

He tried to fall sleep, but anxiety kept him up. He stared at the shadows in the corners as they crept up, and wondered if they had at last . . . No, he couldn't think that way. She couldn't be *gone*.

He wasn't ready for her to be gone, damn it. It was selfish of him, but maybe he was a selfish guy. If there was a possibility she had moved on to where she needed to be, he knew he should be *happy* for her, but instead he felt empty. She couldn't just be there one day and gone the next.

He leaned back on the bed and shut his eyes, less because he had any hope of sleep and more because he was so tired he couldn't keep them open. It was almost one in the morning.

"*Cooper!*"

He sat up so fast he nearly fell out of bed, just as Samantha tried to fling herself into his arms. It should have been comical the way she bounced off him—but it wasn't. She looked pale and worn and scared. Her entire form seemed gray and insubstantial. He would have held on to her if he could have, but he knew that trying to would only make her disappear.

"I got lost!" she cried. "I was walking in Brent's dreams, and then he woke up suddenly and I fell . . . somewhere . . . and I got lost! Those *things* were there, and they could see me, and they wanted to hurt me . . . *and why can't I cry?* Cooper!"

"Samantha . . ." He didn't know what to say. She was huddled on the floor and he couldn't even help her up.

He sat next to her, a little distance away so he didn't

bump into her and displace her. It was awkward, but it was the best he could do.

"I talked to Brent," he said.

She nodded, her hair—devoid of any extra color, and as plain as her torn jeans and black T-shirt—cascading forward to hide her face.

"He knows someone who might be able to help us. He's telepathic, you know." She looked up at that, the fear still on her face, but now mixed with surprise. "Yeah, it was kind of a shock for me, too," Cooper added. "Maybe that's how he could see you in the library, or how you could talk to him in his dreams. You can't normally do that, can you?"

"I don't know. It was the first time I tried it," Samantha mumbled. "He kind of heard me when he was awake. I thought maybe he'd be able to hear better when he was sleeping. I'm not going to do it again, though. It was—" Her breath hitched, but she still couldn't seem to cry. Through all this, her eyes had remained dry.

He put a hand out, and she put one of hers carefully on top of his. He couldn't feel her, and was pretty sure she couldn't feel him, but there was something comforting about at least *trying* to make that kind of contact.

"Brent said this guy he knows believes in magic and supernatural stuff," Cooper said. "He and I are going over there later today. With more people working on it, I'm sure we'll be able to figure out who you are and how to help you."

"A golem?" she said, before sticking out her tongue.

"Who knows?" Cooper watched as her mood lightened, and color literally seeped into her. Green and blue streaks appeared in her hair, and her clothes picked up swirls of color, tonight a fuchsia paisley pattern.

"You look like hell," Samantha observed.

"Yeah," he said, his relief at her reappearance finally allowing his body and mind both to relax.

Samantha looked like she was going to say something sharp—probably complain about his being half conscious after she had had such a scare—so Cooper tried to rouse himself, but instead she just shook her head. "You should lie down. You act like you wish it weren't true some nights, but you keep telling me you need sleep."

He tried to follow her advice. He thought he might even have drifted off and dreamed for a little while, judging by the bitter taste of adrenaline in his mouth when he woke at three-thirty. That's when he gave up, stumbled into the shower, and headed to the shop.

Samantha followed closely. He wasn't even sure she had left his room while he tossed and turned in bed. She obviously didn't want to be alone. He recalled his nightmare from the hospital as he sat at a corner table after his shift, watching people come and go while he waited for Brent. He remembered the dark creatures coming and tearing her into pieces. She had fought to gather herself back together. She had wept then, but now she had no tears.

Had the darkness devoured her tears? Had it taken her memories?

"Hi, Brent," Samantha sighed, causing Cooper to jerk his gaze up. He hadn't noticed Brent come in.

Samantha prepared to scramble out of the way as Brent grabbed the back of her chair and seem poised to sit down.

Instinctively, Cooper said, "Sam's there."

Brent hesitated and looked at the chair, which had to appear empty to him. Then he stepped back, anyway, mumbling awkwardly, "Sorry, Samantha. Um. And good morning."

She waved, but it was obvious Brent couldn't see her as he circled widely around the chair to drag one over from another table.

"Mind if I get a coffee before we go?" Brent asked. "I didn't sleep well."

"Sorry," Cooper said to be polite. Then he realized he probably *was* to blame for Brent's sleepless night. "I'll get it for you. Black, right?"

Brent nodded, again looking around for Samantha.

She waved both hands in front of his eyes, and said, "Anything, Mr. Telepath?"

Cooper left them there and headed behind the counter.

On his way back to Brent, though, he stopped. Those creatures were writhing around under the table, brushing up against Brent's legs like some kind of feral cats. Some had scrambled higher and hooked their claws into Brent's legs, but instead of seeping blood, the wounds emitted a flickering light.

Cooper blinked, and Brent and the table and Samantha were back to normal. Samantha hadn't seemed to see the creatures this time. Brent hadn't even reached to brush them away. Was Cooper hallucinating? Sleeplessness could do that.

He swallowed and forced himself to continue walking calmly toward Brent, who was looking at him with concern.

Cooper handed over the coffee silently. Brent took a sip, then cleared his throat and asked, "What did you see, just then?"

"I don't know."

Samantha frowned. "Was it them again?"

He nodded reluctantly.

"Right," Brent said, "then we should get going."

It took nearly an hour to get to Ryan's house by public transportation, though Cooper suspected it would have been a fifteen-minute ride by car. They had to walk a couple of blocks after the bus let them off in West Roxbury, and when they got to the house, Cooper was ready to keep on walking.

He had expected...well, he wasn't sure. Some little shop with a woman doing tarot readings, or a seedy apartment filled with incense and candles in the windows. West Roxbury had some pretty impressive houses, but Ryan's put the ones around it to shame. It was surrounded by a wrought-iron fence that concealed a large front yard and some kind of funky tree with low, gnarly branches and red leaves.

Brent banged an antique-looking knocker in the shape of a three-headed monster against the door. The sound seemed to echo.

"Is this guy some kind of millionaire?" Cooper asked.

"Inherited money," Brent answered. "He says his family was among the country's founders, and they've done well since. He can be a little arrogant about it, but mostly he just doesn't think in terms of money. It's fun sometimes and annoying at others."

The person who answered the door was not an old-money sorcerer. It was Delilah. She wasn't quite the *last* person on earth Cooper wanted to see, but he wasn't happy about it, either.

"Cooper," Delilah said as she gave him a lazy smile before eyeing Brent coolly. "I overheard someone telling Ryan you two were coming by this morning."

"I . . ." Cooper looked at Brent, feeling both panicked and confused now. "We're just here to . . ."

"I know you're here for Ryan," Delilah said. "If you want me to stick around, Cooper, I can blow off the car wash."

"What are *you* doing here?" Cooper finally managed to blurt out.

"I could ask you the same question, Mr. Dropped-off-the-map-all-summer," Delilah answered with another smile.

"Why don't you answer him first?" Samantha snapped. "And put on some clothes!"

Startled by Samantha's retort, Cooper tried to turn a laugh into a cough. Delilah was wearing *very* short cutoffs and a silky, clinging tank top. It wasn't unusual for her. What was unusual was the fact that she looked toward Samantha at that moment, before turning back to Cooper to say, "If you were coming here for help, I figured there was probably a reason you were avoiding all of us. I thought—"

"Delilah, didn't you say you had a social obligation to attend?" The polished, male voice that came from behind Delilah made Cooper breathe a sigh of relief.

Delilah rolled her eyes. "You sure you don't want me to stick around, Coop?"

"I'll see you later," Cooper replied firmly. He didn't know what she was doing at Ryan's place—maybe there was a perfectly reasonable explanation—but he knew he couldn't handle his old life and this weird, paranormal nightmare mingling just yet.

"I'll hold you to that," she said. "Come by the car wash?"

"Maybe."

"No maybes," Delilah responded. "Just be there. See you, Ryan."

She brushed past him and walked toward the driveway.

"Skank," Samantha mumbled. "Seriously, could she be any more all over you? I thought you said she didn't date football players."

Cooper turned his attention back to the guy who had just greeted him.

Ryan was far from the wizened old man in dusty robes Cooper had pictured when Brent described him. Instead, Ryan seemed to be in his mid-twenties, and though he wore a ring and a necklace, each of a metal darker than silver and inset with arcane symbols, that was the extent of his sorcerer paraphernalia. His hair was dark blond, cut short, his eyes were blue-gray, and he didn't seem to have any piercings or tattoos unless they were hidden by his utterly normal khaki pants and T-shirt. The only thing that struck Cooper was that he was barefoot, but since he was standing in his own house, even that wasn't so strange.

"Sorry about Delilah," Ryan said. "She tends to be more persistent than wise. I take it you're Cooper Blake?" Cooper nodded, and Ryan offered his hand. "Ryan le Coire. Please, come in."

Cooper wondered if he was supposed to introduce Samantha, too. Considering Ryan would learn about her sooner or later, it seemed rude to just ignore her now.

"Can you see—" He broke off, because if Ryan *could* see Samantha, he probably would have spoken to her or at least looked at her since coming to the door.

Brent took over. "Cooper's not the only one looking for help," he explained briefly. "Somewhere around here is Samantha, who, as far as we can tell, is a ghost."

Ryan didn't even blink with surprise. He let out a thoughtful "hmm" and then turned to lead them farther into the house. "We can talk in my study."

Brent followed, and Cooper started to do the same, until he heard Samantha shout, "Hey!" He looked back, and saw her slam her fist into the empty doorway. It bounced back the same way she did when she tried to touch people. "I'm stuck."

Feeling a little crazy talking to a new person this way,

Cooper nevertheless managed to say, "Samantha can't get through the doorway."

"She can come in when I say she can," Ryan said, "and I intend to get a little more information before I extend such an invitation."

"How—"

Ryan cut Cooper off with a wave. "Come upstairs. We'll discuss all this at length." Cooper hesitated, looking back at Samantha, who was frowning, until Ryan added, "Or you could leave. When you make up your mind, Brent knows the way." He walked off, probably perfectly certain that Cooper had to follow, since he wouldn't be here if he didn't need the help.

"I'll be back soon," Cooper said to Samantha.

"Maybe I'll go haunt your girlfriend while you're gone," Samantha replied, pouting.

"I told you, she's not—look, Samantha, I've got to go. Remember this is for your sake, too."

Samantha nodded, but she looked sad and nervous. Cooper didn't want to leave her, especially after seeing the beasts around her again earlier, but what else could he do?

⤝12⤞

Brent watched Cooper look around as they crossed the foyer and climbed the elaborately carved staircase to the second floor. Cooper frowned at the sunlight streaming through windows that appeared to be closely covered from the outside. He stopped on the stairs to stare at the front hall again, and Brent was sure he was doing the same thing everyone did the first time they entered the le Coire manor: mentally measuring the room, and comparing it to the house outside.

The two didn't match.

And Cooper didn't even know about the back garden, where acres of land were hidden inside a tall fence beyond which the world appeared docile and quiet, without a hint of the urban development that existed in the real world.

Cooper's question as they ascended the stairs, however, had nothing to do with any of that.

"You and Delilah know each other?"

Brent paused, debating how much detail to go into. His relationship with Delilah had been awkward enough that he didn't enjoy discussing it, but it seemed some explanation was necessary. "We dated for a few months."

"Wow."

Amused by Cooper's apparent awe, Brent repeated, "Wow?"

"I didn't know she dated," Cooper said. "I know a lot of guys who *tried,* and some who managed first dates when she wanted someone to hang on for a party or dance or something, but no one she dated for any length of time." He shook his head. "Nothing personal, but it's kind of as surprising as finding her here. Is she—" Brent couldn't hear Cooper's thoughts as well in le Coire's place, but he could guess what was going through his head as he blushed and asked, "Can she read minds, too?"

"She wishes she could," Brent answered, recalling the many times Delilah had lambasted him about not using his ability to its full potential. "But no, she's more like Ryan. She works with power. In all honesty, after what happened in the library, I thought about just calling her and saying 'He's your friend. You deal with it.' Her magic is more likely to be useful to you than my telepathy."

"Then why didn't you?" Cooper asked, his tone more curious than upset.

"I didn't trust her with you," Brent answered honestly. "She's the one who told Ryan about me, and I'm grateful she did, but I figured out pretty soon that she did it mostly to get back in his good graces. She's reckless with her power and doesn't have any qualms about putting people around her in danger. You're her friend, so it's possible she would be more careful with you, but I'm not really sure how much her friendship means."

"And you and I knew each other so well you decided to protect me?" Cooper joked.

"What can I say? I felt sorry for Samantha, having to spend all her time with you."

Cooper laughed. "We should probably catch up to Ryan."

They dropped the subject, which was good, since Brent didn't think Cooper would take it well if he told him the whole truth: Brent had been fascinated by the rhythm of Cooper's thoughts, so unlike most people he had met. Once he learned the whole story of his accident, that interest had turned to pity, and a sense of obligation. Cooper didn't seem like the type who wanted to be pitied.

Ryan's study was the only room on the second floor of the le Coire manor Brent had ever been allowed to enter. On the far wall were bookshelves with locking frosted-glass doors. Brent had seen them opened once or twice, but only by Ryan. No one came into this room without his permission. Like the front door, the magic of the house itself enforced that rule.

Aside from a massive mahogany desk with a black ink blotter and a collection of pens—ranging from disposable ballpoints, tossed casually on the desktop, to glass dip-pens and gold fountain pens carefully set in velvet holders—the room held a forest-green suede couch with a matching armchair, and end tables with ivory and jade inlay beneath their glass tops. Ryan had already settled himself in the high-backed leather desk chair, while Cooper froze like a deer in headlights. Brent knew he had done the same the first time he had walked into this house last winter—it felt more like a museum than a place people lived in—but now he just settled comfortably on the couch. Cooper finally perched awkwardly on the opposite side of the couch, seeming too tense to lean back.

"Glad you decided to join me," Ryan said as he pulled a notebook from one of the desk drawers, picked up one of the ballpoint pens, and said simply, "Now, what's going on?"

Cooper rubbed the back of his neck anxiously. "I feel insane even talking about it."

Ryan took a slow breath. "Cooper. I don't care if you're insane. Often the mad have powers the rest of us can hardly comprehend. That being said, I sensed *something* out on that doorstep. You called it a ghost. Such creatures, as popular media has portrayed them, do not exist, but there are plenty of other beings in this world who might imitate a person for their own reasons. Most of them aren't friendly, and many of them can kill a human being through their sheer presence. So I'll repeat the question. What's going on?"

Cooper visibly bristled, his spine straightening and his expression cooling. "Samantha *is* a person, and she would never hurt me."

Brent realized he probably hadn't adequately prepared Cooper for Ryan's style. Then again, there probably *was* no way to prepare someone for Ryan le Coire.

"All right," Ryan answered. "Then you're all set. No problem. You can show yourself out."

"Brent . . . ?" Cooper said, imploring him to help.

Brent would have liked to say, *Don't drag me into this,* but he was the one who had brought Cooper here in the first place.

"Just tell Ryan what's going on," he said instead. "He can probably help, but only if you bother to make an effort."

Cooper obviously had to bite back a rude retort before he said, "Fine. I've been seeing a ghost. Her name's Samantha. She doesn't remember who she was, but she looks around my age and seems local."

Brent noticed that Ryan hadn't written a thing down yet, and knew that meant that so far, Cooper hadn't said anything Ryan thought mattered.

"When did you first see her?"

Cooper tensed. Brent took a deep breath, now glad the powers in the house shielded him from Cooper's thoughts.

"A few months ago," Cooper answered.

"Anything particular happen then?"

This time, when Cooper froze, Brent took pity on him. "He was in a car accident. A nasty one."

"How nasty?"

Cooper swallowed heavily before saying, "It was a close call for me. Other people died." He added quickly, "Two men. No one who was killed was anything like Samantha."

Ryan nodded slightly. "Anything else unusual since the accident?"

"Like what?" Cooper asked nervously.

Brent rested his head on the back of the couch and closed his eyes. Ryan would get Cooper to the answer eventually.

"Okay, fine," Cooper admitted. "I sometimes . . . I don't know how to describe it. Sometimes something happens, and people around me . . . I don't know what happens. Brent, can you help me out? You have more experience with this stuff."

Brent thought back, trying to remember exactly how he felt when Cooper had panicked in the library and seemed to throw him across the room. Instead of describing the sensations out loud, though, he put them together like a package, focusing until they became clear enough for Ryan to pick up on them.

He knew when Ryan had, because his eyes widened, and he said, "Well, that's more interesting than Cooper's . . . ghost, and might be the beginning of an explanation."

"What?" Cooper asked.

Ryan didn't bother to explain, just said bluntly, "I need to know more about the accident."

"I don't remember most of it," Cooper said softly. "I was driving. Then I woke up in the hospital."

"Any dreams?"

Brent winced, as *something* from Cooper's mind got past le Coire's shields. "Ryan—" he started to protest, but Ryan cut him off with a sharp look.

"You *do* remember the accident," Ryan said. "You're just too afraid to admit it. And I would bet you remember more, from when you were unconscious in the hospital."

"I never said I was unconscious."

"I'm not an idiot," Ryan replied, standing to walk around the desk. "You said it was a close call. You would have been out for a while. What did you see then?"

"I don't remember!" Cooper snapped.

"Ryan!" Brent shouted, this time more assertively.

Cooper had taken a step back.

"Were you the one driving?" Ryan asked, glancing at the notebook in his hand as he closed the distance between them again. "More important, were you the one who caused the accident?"

Cooper lifted his hands to push Ryan away. Brent tried to slam into place every mental shield he had, not wanting to experience this aspect of Cooper's power again.

Ryan caught Cooper's wrists. The instant they touched, the air gave a concussive shudder, and Cooper wobbled, stumbling back; Brent jumped up to stabilize him, while Ryan jotted something down in his notebook.

As Brent deposited a semiconscious Cooper on the

couch, Ryan leaned back on the desk, and said, "That was pretty much what I expected."

"What...wha—" Cooper opened his eyes, and his mumbled question was replaced by a wheezing gasp and a wash of fear so strong it knocked Brent to his knees despite Ryan's magic. Cooper's face was pale and his lips looked blue.

Brent was concerned the former football player was about to pass out until Ryan stepped forward with a sigh. He fearlessly touched Cooper's shoulder, and said, "They came in with you. Many more of them would have come in, had I let your Samantha through the doorway. I can banish them for now, but they'll find you again once you leave here."

"What...are...they?" Cooper whispered, his eyes still darting around the room.

"In brief, they're vermin," Ryan answered nonchalantly. "They have no particular goal except to feed, which they do upon the power put out by emotions like pain and fear. A healthy human being has natural defenses against the vermin of the paranormal world, but injury or trauma can make a person vulnerable, allowing vermin not only to feed but to heighten the person's negative emotions. The only remotely interesting thing about your case is that, with this many around you and no experience dealing with them, you should have descended into complete madness by now, unable to even step outside your own door. You might think your memories of the accident are stressful, but with so many scavengers magnifying and feeding on that terror, I'm surprised you're not reliving the experience in your head every moment of every day."

Brent shuddered, remembering the creatures he had seen in the library, in the shadows as he tried to sleep, and in his dream with Samantha. How many of them was Cooper seeing now? How many had been around them both all this time?

≶13≷

Delilah stretched out, sunbathing on the hood of her car, as the figure Cooper had called Samantha kicked repeatedly at the door to le Coire's house. She had walked through Ryan's bushes—literally *through* them, without disturbing a branch, bird or squirrel—and tried to peer through the windows before pounding her fists against the glass.

When Samantha's hands had struck the edges of the le Coire manor, where Ryan's magic gave off hot sparks, her form seemed to dissolve.

Delilah yawned and rubbed her temples. After learning Cooper would be here today, she had spent much of last night preparing, so she would be able to see the power connected to him more clearly. Doing so had left her exhausted, and watching Samantha now made her eyes water.

Instead of a solid body, Samantha deemed to be made up of bright colors in a vaguely human-shaped form that glistened and wavered as if reflected on the surface of a rapidly moving river. Delilah's eyes couldn't quite focus on it.

Samantha paced around the house for the second time now before she turned, frustrated, and then paused, apparently noticing Delilah.

"Hello," Delilah said.

Samantha hesitated. Delilah had been more focused on Cooper and hadn't heard everything Samantha said about her earlier, but she had not been unaware of the creature's hostility. She was also, unfortunately, aware of the shadows that rose and pressed against her shields as soon as Cooper's "ghost" turned toward her.

Keeping herself protected from the scavengers, but open enough to outside power to see Samantha, required maintaining a precarious balance. Delilah wasn't sure she could do it for long. She only hoped she could convince Samantha to come somewhere safe with her.

"There's not much use in trying to get inside," Delilah said, speaking softly. "The le Coire family is strictly devoted to helping *humans*. If Ryan invites you in, it will be because he thinks he can control you and use you."

Samantha's response was indignant. "I *am* human," she protested. Her voice was haunting and powerful, like the bone-deep quiver left behind by a roll of thunder. Surely this wasn't how Cooper perceived the creature, or he would have run away long ago. "Or, I was."

"I heard Brent say you're a ghost?" Delilah may have left when Ryan told her to, but that didn't mean she wasn't allowed to stay in the front yard and eavesdrop.

"Aren't you a *cheerleader?*" Samantha asked. "Don't tell me you're from some kind of ancient line of sorcerers, too?"

Delilah noted Samantha's use of the word *sorcerer,* instead of the more common term *witch.* Witches were born or created with their magic tied into their blood; they needed to do nothing more than survive in order to maintain it. Sorcerers, on the other hand, spent their lives devoted to studying the workings of power and building their own. Brent tended to misuse the word *witch* to refer to anyone with power, so he would not have taught her the difference. And Cooper certainly wouldn't know it.

It could be mere coincidence that Samantha used the right word, or it could mean she knew more than she seemed to.

Instead of challenging the supposed ghost, Delilah laughed, preferring to seem harmless. "Yes, I'm a cheerleader, and no, I'm the child of two parents with no magical background whatsoever. But I have studied intensively on my own almost since grade school. I met Ryan a few years ago, after I had what he would refer to as an 'amateur's accident.' One that nearly killed me."

She added the last bit on a gamble. This creature could be very, *very* dangerous . . . or she could be exactly what she said she was, in which case Delilah might be able to win some of her trust by communicating honestly.

"Oh?"

Delilah thought she detected genuine curiosity. "I ran afoul of those . . . *things*," she said, reluctant to describe the shadows in more detail until she found out more about Samantha. "The ones I see all around you and Cooper. I had been able to see them for a long time, but I didn't know how to protect myself from them until Ryan taught me how."

That caught Samantha's attention, and she being began to move closer. Delilah had to shift her gaze away, unable to watch her walk without experiencing vertigo. "Can you destroy them?"

"There's no point in trying to destroy them," Delilah said. It was the truth, but it also meant she didn't need to admit the limits of her own power. "There are always more."

"If there are so many of them, why don't they bother everyone?"

"The average person just isn't worth hunting," Delilah explained, an answer straight out of the le Coire family textbook—if they believed in putting such information down on paper. "The human body blocks power both ways, keeping magic in, but outside powers out, like a shell protecting a nut. To use magic, you have to reach past your own skin. That means gathering more power than most people have, which makes you tastier, and then giving up your primary defense. The first time I successfully raised enough magic to do something impressive, when I was twelve, a bunch of those shadow-things swarmed at me. I ended up having to tell people at school I had mono, it took that long for me to get any strength back."

"I bet Cooper was worried," Samantha said.

Delilah chuckled. This time it was genuine and not just an attempt to be disarming. "You're sweet on him, aren't you?"

"Am not," Samantha retorted.

"Look, it's okay," Delilah assured her. "Cooper Blake is absolutely *not* my type. I care about him. He's a friend and, of course, he's on my team, too. But I like a guy with a little more spine and a little more . . . pizzazz."

"He's been good to me," Samantha said softly. "He's trying to help me."

"Yeah, he's in the wrong place for that," Delilah scoffed. "Look, Ryan works well with humans, and—" She broke off when Samantha started to object again. "Maybe you used to be human. But you're not anymore. I can respect you as a *person*—which is more than I can say for Ryan— but don't expect me to treat you like you're a regular human being with no unusual features. If nothing else you're a little mortality-challenged."

"I think I got the mortality thing down pretty well," Samantha replied hotly. "It's kind of requisite to dying, right?"

Delilah wasn't cut out to be a teacher. She didn't have the patience for it. *Mortal* and *immortal* meant different things in this context than they did in a biology class.

"When you're dealing with power, it's a technical term. Mortality is what gives you the ability to touch things. It's flesh and blood."

"And you lose it when you die?"

Delilah was pretty certain that you lose *everything* when you die except the would-be dust the body was made of, but didn't think Samantha was the type to accept that as a response. "Yeah," she replied. "And normally when humans lose that, the scavengers eat what's left."

Samantha moved again. She seemed to be sitting on the car hood next to Delilah, which Delilah preferred; it took less effort to see her out of the corner of the eye than it did to look at her straight on. The power she put out from this close, though, caused gooseflesh to raise on Delilah's arms.

"How long?" Samantha asked, her voice not exactly deeper, but darker. Was she frightened?

Delilah blinked, distracted by the cold power washing past her. "How long what?"

"Until they finish me off," Samantha said.

"Oh." Delilah hadn't expected Samantha to seem so *sincere.* "Well . . . I mean, if you were really just human, they would have done it pretty much instantly."

"Then what am I? And why don't I remember? I don't have any memories from before Cooper opened his eyes in that hospital."

Delilah shifted uncomfortably. The last thing she had expected was to feel sorry for this creature. She had thought that maybe she could disconnect Samantha from Cooper, and use Samantha for her own means, the same way Ryan probably planned to. Delilah didn't think of herself as overly burdened with protective instincts, but she couldn't help but feel some pity at Samantha's plight.

"I don't know what you are," she answered truthfully. "If you don't have mortal power, and you haven't been devoured by the shadows, then you have immortal power. It's kind of an either/or thing. As for why you don't remember your life before this, I don't have an answer. Most immortals are these awesome, scary-as-hell, godlike creatures. People risk everything to summon them with sacrifices of blood and flesh and vows in order to gain incredible power. My best guess is that you were someone who did something like that—like the sorcerers in Ryan's line, nominally human but with a *lot* of power. Maybe you had enough immortal power so that when you died, you could hold on to this world even without your body."

Samantha seemed to consider that for a while, but then she sighed. "I remember how to play hopscotch," she said. "I remember the theme song of *The Twilight Zone*. I remember all the words to the national anthem. If I were a sorcerer, shouldn't I remember *something* about magic?"

Delilah sat back with a *humph*. "Good point." So far, the only indication Delilah had that Samantha might know anything about magic was her probably random use of the correct word. "Look . . ." Delilah paused, but not for long. Certainly not long enough to avoid a blistering lecture from Ryan later if something went wrong. "No matter what you *are,* we know what you need, right?"

"A pony?"

Delilah should have seen that one coming.

"You need mortal power."

"Can I find that at Target?" Samantha asked, her voice dripping with sarcasm. "Or is it more of a special-order item?"

The idea that Samantha had once been a sorcerer seemed less likely with every passing moment, but that didn't matter to Delilah anymore.

"Like I said, the greater immortals get their mortal forms by making deals with humans." And the human sorcerers involved in those deals usually got incredible power as a result, including, but not limited to, the possibility of living forever. "Come with me. I can put up a protective circle to keep the scavengers away from both of us for a little while, and we'll see about giving you a little of my mortality. Enough to let you protect yourself from the shadows, and maybe let you form a solid body for yourself."

"You would do that for me?"

So naïve, Delilah thought. Samantha had no idea what Delilah could possibly gain from such an exchange. "I'm up for an adventure if you are," she answered.

14

Cooper's head was spinning, but he wasn't sure whether it was the result of what Ryan had *done,* or what he was still saying.

The doctors had told Cooper that his survival after the accident had been a miracle. Now, Ryan was telling him his continued existence was equally mysterious. How could it suddenly be so eerie to be alive?

He looked to Brent for some kind of support, but the telepath had curled up in a chair across the room and seemed to be trying to figure out what Cooper had seen. Cooper envied him that particular blindness.

"So, if the shadows are a symptom, not the problem, then what's the problem?" Cooper asked.

"Well, you have two," Ryan answered. "The first is that you're not well-connected to your flesh, and have the ability to disconnect other people from theirs. The skin is a human's primary defense against the scavengers, so stepping outside it gives them ample opportunity to feed. If it weren't above their capacity for reason, I would suggest they may be keeping you alive because you're likely to deliver them other meals."

"Not likely," Cooper mumbled. Why would he want to give them anything?

"Accidentally," Ryan clarified. "Delilah and Brent both have more than their fair share clinging to them." Cooper saw Brent look up swiftly, eyes wide, before Ryan continued. "Luckily, they're both stable enough not to be in too much danger. However, I suspect you've infected almost everyone you've been in contact with since the accident."

Cooper shuddered at the thought. "Most of the time they don't even bother me," he insisted. "I see them when I try to sleep or something, but not much otherwise."

"Most of the time, you aren't *able* to see them," Ryan said. "It takes intense training or a dreadful mistake for a human to be able to see creatures of raw power, like the beasts hunting you. In your case, you can see them when you're partially outside your flesh."

The concept made Cooper shudder, but he tried to stay focused. "What's the other problem?"

"Samantha," Ryan answered bluntly. "She's not a ghost. Human ghosts don't exist. I can't say for certain what she *is*, except that she is obviously associated with the scavengers and closely linked to you. The beasts that cling to you don't have the intelligence to make a plan, or keep their host alive for their long-term benefit, but there *are* creatures that do possess such a capacity. Samantha might be one of them."

Cooper shook his head at the implication. "You don't know Samantha. She's lonely and scared, not some kind of evil parasite."

"If we stop to assume for a moment that Samantha is a human ghost," Ryan said slowly, "what did you want from me?"

Somehow, the question surprised Cooper, though it was an entirely reasonable one. He couldn't answer right away. What *had* he hoped for? He suspected he had clung to Brent's company for reassurance that he wasn't in fact crazy. Brent had said that Ryan could help, and Cooper had gone with him, wanting help . . . but with what, if not just further validation?

"I want to help Samantha," he said out loud, though even that was vague and, of course, Ryan caught on to that ambiguity right away.

"You want to help her," Ryan said. "How? If she is in fact a ghost, if she is in fact *dead,* then how do you intend to help her? Would you bring her back to life if you had the ability? Even if she died in a pretty fashion, according to your tale she's been gone for months. Her body is not going to be in good shape. She might need to acquire another one—"

"No, no, nothing like that," Cooper protested, repulsed by the image of a Samantha who had been left to rot for months, with her long blond hair pooling in fluids of decay.

"If she is a ghost," Ryan said, continuing inexorably, "then it's likely that whatever else is left of her is in a box somewhere. If you're not discussing resurrection or possession, then you're talking about exorcism. If you want me to banish her—or, more gently, I could say 'to send her on'—then I could almost certainly do that."

"But you already said that ghosts like her don't exist, so how can you propose to do anything like that?" Cooper challenged.

Ryan shrugged enigmatically. "Whether she's a ghost or something else, she doesn't have a mortal form, and that makes her vulnerable. In the field of psychic arm wrestling, I almost always win. I usually prefer to understand something before I banish it, especially when dealing with apparently sentient beings, but I'm offering scenarios here."

"And if she's one of those *other* things you talked about, what will happen to her?"

"Oh, *now* you're willing to consider it?" Ryan asked. Cooper was pretty sure he had just fallen into a really obvious verbal trap. "I think, Cooper, that you should take some time to sort out what you want. Do you want the truth and to help Samantha, or do you want to comfort yourself? If it's the latter, is having her around and dealing with her mystery more comforting to you than letting her go would be?"

Of *course* he wanted to help Samantha, but if she was really a ghost, that would mean allowing her to be dead.

He remembered what Ryan had said about the shadows

making painful emotions worse. Maybe, without them, he and Samantha would be in better shape, and could take care of their own problems.

"You said my first problem was my not being attached to my body right or something, which attracts the shadows," he said, trying to circle back to a simpler part of the conversation. "Can you help me solve that issue? I mean, if you're right, and Samantha is . . . something else, something bad . . . then if I fix my shadow problem, she won't have any use for me, right? And if she stays around after they're gone, then she probably *isn't* using me the way you think she might be, and we can explore other options."

Ryan smiled again. It was patronizing, and it kind of made Cooper want to hit him.

"If that's the plan," Cooper said when it became obvious that Ryan was waiting for him to continue, "then I guess it would help to know how this happened in the first place? I mean, I didn't just pick up magic powers out of nowhere, right?"

Ryan's indulgent smile was replaced by a wince. "Your ability isn't a 'magic power,' " Ryan said. "For human beings to gain real *power*, they need to make deals. They need to work with beings a little less human than those of us in this room. Your little trick? It's more like a reflex. You probably learned it in the accident. It's no more inhuman than Brent's telepathy, or—"

"How do you pick up telepathy as a reflex?" Cooper interrupted.

"Just like any other one," Ryan replied vaguely. "May I demonstrate?"

"Um . . . okay?"

He had barely spoken the words before Ryan's fist came up and caught him square on the jaw. It wasn't nearly as hard a blow as Cooper had received on the football field, but he was completely unprepared for it, and it sent him stumbling back toward the couch.

"What the hell was *that* for?" he demanded.

"You said I could demonstrate."

"I didn't—" Okay, he did, and should have known better, given how many times Ryan had already pushed his buttons. "I didn't mean—"

"The point would have been lost if I explained ahead of time," Ryan said before, incredibly, he tried it *again*.

Still wound up from the first blow, and watching Ryan a good deal more carefully now, Cooper managed to dodge this one—and throw a right hook back at him. But Ryan just stepped into Cooper's punch and, instead of getting hit, somehow sent Cooper sailing back to the couch again, where he lay, disoriented, while Ryan kept talking.

"Human beings learn quickly to avoid and respond to things that might hurt them," Ryan said. "It's simple. We pick up cues that warn us of approaching danger. We become more sensitive to those cues when we *know* we're in danger. And when we find a way to defend ourselves, we use it instinctively."

Cooper rubbed his jaw, still wondering how this guy who looked like a college kid and spoke like some kind of professor had managed to knock him off his feet twice in the same afternoon.

"Now," Ryan said, continuing, "I'll give you the same option I gave Brent when he first came here. I can help you clamp down so hard on your ability you'll never reach it again, or I can teach you to use it as you choose, instead of just lashing out with it in a blind panic. Either way, in the process you'll learn how to keep yourself contained when you need to be, so the scavengers can't make a meal out of you."

"I appreciate the offer," Cooper grumbled, "but . . . first, two more questions. If you're saying these abilities are developed through some kind of protective response, then why is mine putting me in danger? Brent said his telepathy put him in the hospital."

"Because sometimes your body makes mistakes. It's a bad idea to shut your eyes when something flies at your windshield while you're driving, or to freeze in place in the middle of the street when a truck is about to run you over, right? But people still do it. That's why we need to make a conscious effort to control our responses."

Cooper knew there was sometimes a difference between what your body wanted you to do, and what you needed to do, especially when it came to football, where he had trained himself to hold on to the ball, even if it meant falling on his face.

"Next question," he said. "How do I put this? You're kind of an asshole. Why do you want to help me at all?"

"I told you," Ryan said, a hint of frustration in his tone.

"Possessing real magic involves making deals with powers beyond your current comprehension. My family made those agreements centuries ago, and we have been sorcerers and scholars ever since. The le Coire family is the oldest and most powerful human line on this continent to ever study these magics. I believe, as did most of my ancestors, that our power isn't just a gift to be squandered. I don't have to like you, and vice versa, for me to have an obligation to offer to teach you. Whether you say yes is up to you."

Cooper hesitated. He knew he needed to learn what Ryan had to teach, if only to prove that Samantha wasn't evil, and to convince Ryan to help *her,* somehow, too. He just didn't like the idea of spending more time with him.

"Take a day," Ryan suggested. "Ask Brent and Delilah what it's like to study with me. Look around and see if you can recognize which people near you have your shadows clinging to them, and how it's affecting them. And," he concluded with a cool smile, "maybe you should see what Samantha thinks of the plan." He shrugged. "Or maybe you shouldn't. If she *is* the one keeping you alive, and she thinks you might not be useful anymore, it could end badly. Either way, be here tomorrow morning if you want my help."

Cooper wanted to defend Samantha again, but couldn't seem to find the words as a shiver ran down his spine.

15

Cooper rubbed his jaw as he and Brent climbed onto the train going back to town. "I'm wondering if Ryan and I would both survive it, if I accept his offer to teach me anything."

"I don't know of anyone who's died there yet," Brent assured him. "Ryan is always pretty abrasive, but he gets easier to work with once he believes that you're willing to put in the effort."

"How hard is it to convince him of that?"

Brent seemed to ponder that one for quite a while, before saying, "As you might have guessed, you're not the first person to try to hit him. I've never seen anyone connect, though I tried my best. More importantly, I've never seen Ryan get angry about it. He says that it's easiest for most people to tap into their power when their emotions are running high, so I think he baits people on purpose."

"Oh, fun," Cooper grumbled.

"Speaking of which, is Samantha angry about being locked out?"

Cooper nodded. "She said she was going to follow Delilah, so she's probably at the car wash now." He wasn't sure what to make of her abrupt about-face on her opinion of Delilah. Was she as unsettled as he was by finding Delilah at Ryan's?

"Do you want to swing by after we get back to town?" Brent asked. "I think the flyers I saw said the car wash would run until five, so we could get there half an hour or so before they shut down."

"I don't know," Cooper said. "If Ryan's right, my being around them could hurt the other guys, too, couldn't it?"

"I don't know," Brent said, before he blurted out, "You have to have *some* thoughts on what Ryan said about Samantha. What if she *isn't* what you think she is? Maybe she isn't even what *she* thinks she is, and that's why you two haven't been able to figure out *who* she is."

"I just don't believe she would hurt anyone," Cooper said, recalling too vividly how scared Samantha had seemed after having been "lost" last night. No matter what Ryan said, Cooper had a hard time believing it was really all an act.

Of course, her fear made him more afraid, which was what those shadow-creatures were supposed to—

No. He didn't believe that. Even if Ryan was right and Samantha couldn't be a ghost, that didn't mean she was evil. Maybe Samantha didn't mean to lie to anyone, but was deceiving herself, like Brent said.

Despite his reservations, when they left the train, Cooper found himself heading toward the grocery store parking lot where he knew the team would be. He wanted to see Samantha again to make sure she was all right.

And he wanted to see the guys. He had been so nervous about even calling them all summer, but if part of that nervousness had been caused by the shadows, then he should seize the moment before they came back. Ryan had said that healthy people weren't at risk, so Cooper didn't think he'd actually be endangering them. He would say a quick hello, and hopefully find Samantha in the process.

Brent was following quietly beside him, "Going to check out the car wash after all?"

"I guess I am," he said. "I mean, I should, right?" He felt as if he could breathe easier than he had been able to in months.

Brent shrugged. "You want company or should I ditch?"

"Would it be absolutely pathetic if I asked you to come?" Cooper asked. John had seemed willing to forgive and forget that he had abandoned him for months, but their conversation had still been awkward even before the shadows came. Cooper didn't know how the rest of the team would react. They had a right to be pissed at him.

"No problem," Brent said. "I can provide an excuse and drive the getaway car if we need to make our escape."

Cooper laughed a little at the image, but it was mostly forced.

John looked up just then and did a double take. Cooper froze like a rabbit as the 227-pound linebacker ran at him. If John actually hit him with any force, he was going to go down, *hard,* before John even realized that Cooper had lost most of the bulk and muscle that would enable him to meet that kind of greeting.

Thankfully, John stopped, grinning, a couple feet in front of Cooper. If the shadows that had harassed John back at school had done any damage, it didn't show.

"It's good to see you up and about and not looking like hell," John said bluntly, his smile not fading.

"Yeah. I'm sorry I haven't called or anything."

"I figured you'd get in touch when you felt up to it. I told the guys to leave you alone until then . . . though I don't suppose you'll be coming back to the team?"

Cooper shook his head, relief at the warm greeting actually making his head spin. When the doctors had first told him that it was a very bad idea for him to go back to football, it had seemed like a death knell. Now, months later, he managed to smile as he said, "I'm going to have to watch this season."

"Well, you two look like you need to catch up," Brent said, apparently having decided he had stood awkwardly nearby long enough. "I'm going to bail. Unless you still need help with that thing, Cooper?"

Cooper recognized the offer as an excuse to leave, in case he needed or wanted it, and was grateful.

"You should stick around, Coop," John said. "Hang with us. We're all going over to the beach after we're done here if the weather holds, and then we're going to hit Frank's Grill for dinner."

Cooper was shaking his head before he even realized it. "I've got work in the morning," he said, even though he knew perfectly well that his father would let him off work in a heartbeat if he asked, and his mother would be delighted he was going out with the guys from the team. Unless he could find a swimsuit that didn't show his arms, torso, or legs, he wouldn't be hitting the beach anytime soon. Maybe someday, but he wasn't quite ready to show off the extent of the damage to the world yet.

"C'mon," John said. "You can come out for a while. Who needs sleep, right? You don't even need to do suicide drills at practice tomorrow. You can handle—"

"I can't," Cooper said, more sharply than he had intended.

John went quiet.

"Sorry, man," Cooper said, dropping his head as he tried to push back the anxiety that was starting to spike again. "I'm still a little . . . off. I don't know. Say hi to the guys for me, though?"

"Say hi to them yourself?" John suggested, gesturing over his shoulder to the rest of the team, who were manning the car wash when they weren't glancing not entirely subtly over at John, Cooper and Brent. Delilah wasn't with them; either she had decided not to come back to the car wash, or she was promoting the car wash somewhere else.

Cooper was glad not to have to face her again yet, but disappointed to see that Samantha wasn't here, either.

"Might as well say hello," Brent encouraged him.

Cooper looked skeptically, wondering if Brent was trying to help or get rid of him.

John seemed equally confused, as if he were trying to figure out who Brent was and why he was involved. "Do I know you?" he asked.

"I went to a couple parties with Delilah," Brent answered with a sigh.

"Oh," John said, his eyes widening in surprise. "Well. Um. Huh."

"Let's go say hi," Cooper said, changing the subject. Cooper wondered how recently Brent and Delilah had broken up, and what she had been saying to the guys since.

He started across the parking lot, acutely aware that the rest of the team had dropped any attempt at discretion and had turned to smile at him. He tried to remind himself that these were his *friends,* and not to be feared.

But when Reggie, one of the biggest guys on the team, clapped him on the shoulder, he remembered one of the reasons why he had avoided these friends in the first place. The friendly gesture, once so familiar, not only made him stumble but sent a shard of pain from his shoulder, past his once-broken ribs, and into his recently fractured hip.

He managed to bite back what would have been a very

loud curse, but couldn't hide his pain or the way it made his skin pale.

Not all of his issues were supernatural or in his head.

"Oh, God. Sorry, man," Reggie said.

"You okay?" John asked, immediately at his side.

Pity. Yeah, that was the other thing he had really *not* wanted to deal with. Just thinking about it made the world around him seem to darken, and he had a feeling that the shadows had found him.

He took a couple steps backward, trying not to limp but knowing he wasn't completely hiding it.

"Good to see you all," he said, "but I've got to get going."

"Coop, I'm sorry," Reggie said again.

If they had told him to suck it up, be a man, or laughed it off, that would have been normal. Maybe they would even have acted that way if Cooper hadn't brought along his own little cloud of misery.

"It's fine," he answered. "I've just got to go. I'm late."

He didn't say for what, didn't know for what.

"Hey, Cooper," John called as Cooper attempted to walk away with some dignity. "Tomorrow afternoon, my place, opening-season game party. Hope to see you there."

Cooper nodded acknowledgement, but not agreement.

He got out of eyesight of the team, rounding the block, and then had to stop and lean against the building and suck in deep drafts of air. Reggie had managed to hit him just the wrong way.

"Can you get home or back to the shop?" Brent asked him.

He had forgotten Brent was even there.

He started to nod, but then realized the answer was no. "Give me a hand?" he asked.

Brent didn't hesitate, just threw Cooper's arm over his shoulders and helped him limp back toward the shop. "My car's right around here, if you're okay with a short trip."

"No highways?"

"We can do back roads."

"Can you give me a ride home?"

"No problem."

Tomorrow, Cooper knew he would have to swallow his pride and go back to Ryan, and hoped he would learn something useful. He couldn't go on this way.

⚡10⚡

Delilah tried to keep up a cool front, but she was almost as nervous as she was excited. The warded circle she had created in the woods kept the scavengers out, but that wouldn't matter if she had misjudged and Samantha was actually malevolent. Then the instant Delilah summoned power and lowered her defenses, Samantha could just reach in and hollow Delilah out, stealing power and mind and leaving Delilah's body an empty shell.

She had just pressed her hand to the edge of the circle when Samantha, still locked outside for the moment, asked, "How powerful *are* you, anyway?"

Truth? Lie? Bluffing about the strength of her abilities might make her seem too dangerous for Samantha to mess with. On the other hand, if Samantha was really as powerful as Delilah thought she could be, then she might know perfectly well that she could overpower any first-generation sorcerer, in which case it would be more valuable to downplay her own power and its worth.

"Powerful enough that I think I can help you," she finally answered.

With a tight breath, she parted the edge of the circle. Samantha did not wait to be invited forward. It took some effort to let Samantha in while keeping the pacing scavengers around her out where they were harmless, but Delilah managed.

She turned her eyes from the shadows and back to Samantha, and jumped with surprise. Inside her own circle, Delilah could see Samantha more easily and more clearly. She understood now why Cooper had been convinced his ghost was harmless.

Samantha—no, the *illusion* Samantha projected—was a couple of inches shorter than Delilah. Her hair and clothing were a style that could best be described as punk or scene, with bright, mismatched colors. Her faded blue jeans with splashes of pastel orange and pink paint had enough holes in them to reveal the green-and-yellow paisley tights she was wearing underneath. Her T-shirt was neon purple, with a cute line-art version of the Lenmark Ocelots' logo. Delilah was pretty sure that if she copied it, she could get all the girls on the squad to buy one.

Delilah shook her head, trying to get some sense back in it. Samantha chewed on a lock of her blond hair as Delilah opened the cooler she kept her tools in. She used to keep them in the house, but after her mother confiscated sage for the fourth time and then had Delilah take a drug test, Delilah decided her tools should be a bit more hidden. Unfortunately, she couldn't explain to her mother—who *still* called John's mother before every game party to ensure adequate supervision—that she had a better use for spices than cooking.

"So," Samantha said. "What do we do now?"

Delilah was wondering that herself. "Well, step one, we're going to need to figure out what kind of power you have. Immortal power is sometimes called elemental power, since it tends to fall into one of four forms: earth, air, fire, and water. They link in different ways to mortal power."

She wasn't sure why her voice was wavering.

Suddenly, a piece of advice Ryan had once given her came to mind: *When you find yourself about to raise power, and you realize your heart is racing and you're shaking and pale, stop. We have instincts for a reason. They warn us when, for example, something is trying to eat us.*

"What's wrong?" Samantha asked.

Delilah looked beyond the circle again. Of course she felt hunted; the shadows were thicker out there now, swarming and hungry. But they couldn't get in, and after this, hopefully Delilah would have the power to banish them forever instead of just holding them at arm's length.

"How dangerous is this for you?" Samantha asked when Delilah still hadn't responded.

Delilah shrugged, trying to appear nonchalant. "I know what I'm doing." She *did*. "I'm going to start with fire, since that tends to be the most common and the easiest to invoke."

Samantha nodded, once again sucking on her hair. She looked nervous, which actually made Delilah feel better.

Delilah took a deep breath, and then began building the fire. That was the easy part; she had a basin in the circle, along with kindling and small logs kept dry under a tarp. She kindled a small but steady flame, and then stared for a couple seconds at the very sharp edge of her pocketknife. Fire elementals were bound in blood, which meant that's what she'd need to offer to invoke them.

She could always tell the girls on the squad she cut herself during set construction, and tell her friends in the drama department she hurt herself during cheerleading practice.

She set the knife on the upper side of her arm. The cut hurt more than it would have on the fleshy side, but it would suck to accidentally send herself to the hospital trying to become immortal.

Holding her arm above the fire, low enough to feel the heat but far enough away not to get instantly burned, she focused her power into the blood and spread her attention to Samantha, trying to detect any change—

The instant her blood and the fire touched, the fire flared so high that Delilah had to fling herself backward to avoid the flames. Simultaneously, she heard Samantha cry out, and watched in shock as the fire collapsed into itself with a *whumph* that made the edges of the circle shudder. All that was left behind was cold, black ash.

For an instant, Samantha's form rippled and darkened. When she solidified again, she looked frightened. She crossed her arms tightly across her chest, and her clothing had become monochromatic.

"What was that?" she whispered.

"A response," Delilah replied, though she wasn't quite sure what kind. It wasn't what she had expected. "Are you all right?"

Samantha hesitated before nodding. "I guess so. I don't think I like fire."

Delilah looked up as a raindrop fell on her head. "That's good, since it looks like the weather isn't going to let us try that one again." She was about to suggest that maybe they should go inside until the weather had cleared when the obvious occurred to her.

The rain wasn't a coincidence.

In fact, she suspected she knew the reason why the entire summer had been unusually wet.

Ryan said that water was the hardest of the elemental powers to invoke or control. Water-based powers were bound in tears, and therefore usually came from grief.

From death.

If Samantha's element was water, that would explain why she had appeared after a devastating accident that had caused two deaths. It would explain why she had attached herself to an individual who was experiencing so much pain and frustration.

It also meant Samantha was far, *far* more powerful than she could possibly know. Delilah had assumed that Samantha was the remains of a sorcerer who had found a way to survive death, but even Ryan could not manipulate weather without an incredible amount of ritual and energy.

But Samantha wasn't a ghost, or a sorcerer, or any kind of human being that was or ever had been. She *was* power—pure, elemental energy, formed out of human deaths, but without enough mortality to make the shape solid.

Did Samantha know? That was the question. Elemental powers were not self-aware until someone called upon them and gave them will and purpose. It was possible Samantha didn't remember her history because she had none.

Fog.

Delilah remembered the way the papers described the thick, blinding fog that had caused devastation on an otherwise normal highway.

"Delilah?" Samantha's voice was soft, troubled. "What happened? Did something go wrong? Are you all right?"

Delilah nodded.

"Yeah. I figured out what I needed to," she managed to say.

"You look scared."

Did she dare go through with this?

Did she dare *not*? No sorcerer had ever bound to and worked with water. It didn't usually respond well enough to human will to be commanded. But here was Samantha, seemingly willing to cooperate. The chance of Delilah ever again encountering a creature like this, who was apparently ignorant of its own nature, was nil.

If Samantha was lying, then Delilah was probably courting a quick and painful death. But if Samantha simply had no idea what was going on, then Delilah could gain power beyond even le Coire's dreams, all in the guise of trying to help her. After all, water was the most abundant elemental force on Earth, with the ability to douse any of the others.

She would be a fool not to risk it.

⚡17⚡

The car ride home was short, and set Cooper's heart to pounding, but he managed. That alone seemed like a big step.

By the time Brent pulled up to his house, Cooper felt able to walk on his own, but Brent hovered by his side, as if worried Cooper was going to fall over anyway. Cooper would have waved him off, if he hadn't had the same fear.

"Not that I wanted to see Delilah again, but I wonder where she and Samantha ended up," Brent said as they limped up the driveway. "I hope Sam's having fun haunting her."

Maybe . . . maybe not. Cooper bit his tongue rather than mention what had happened to Samantha after she talked to Brent in his sleep.

"She's pissed at me for going into Ryan's when she

couldn't," he said instead. Of course, that was actually *true;* she had seemed cross. It wouldn't be out of character for her to try to make him sweat a little in retaliation. Or maybe she was trying to get Delilah's attention again like she had at the sandwich shop, now knowing that Delilah was mixed up with witchcraft and more likely to be able to see her.

Cooper's mom opened the front door before they reached it, looking alarmed.

"What's wrong?" she asked, coming forward.

"I'm fine," Cooper answered. "Really. I said hi to the guys at the car wash and forgot to warn them to be gentle."

"Really?" she asked, sounding both optimistic and suspicious. "I'm sorry, where are my manners? Cooper, do I know your friend?"

"This is Brent," Cooper said. Normally he would have added something involving "I met him at...," but his mind went blank when he tried. There wasn't a good explanation for why he and Brent started talking that didn't involve ghosts.

"Nice to meet you, ma'am," Brent said, shaking her hand, the picture of what Cooper's mother would call "good breeding."

"Well, come in and sit down, both of you," she said, reaching to give Cooper a hand up the two steps into the front hall.

"I should probably get going, actually," Brent said. "Do you need a ride tomorrow, Cooper?"

Ryan's. Cooper knew he should probably accept a ride. Otherwise, he was likely to chicken out or come up with an excuse to stay away from Ryan le Coire, with his less than gentle teaching methods and distrust of Samantha. "If you don't mind, yeah."

"Are you two going to the game party?" Cooper's mom asked. The opening-season party at John's house had been a tradition for six years now.

Cooper debated the merits of lying, and was grateful when Brent got to the question first. "If we're lucky," he answered, with that same easy, good-boy smile. "The Museum of Science has a special exhibit this weekend that we can get extra credit in our physics class for going to. Since I suck at physics, it seemed worthwhile."

Brent shot him a don't-screw-this-up look, so Cooper added, "Five extra points at the start of the semester seemed like a stupid thing to throw away. Hopefully it won't take too long, and we can get to the game party in time for kickoff."

Cooper's and John's moms talked regularly enough that he was obligated to show up now.

"See you in the morning, Cooper," Brent said, moving into the doorway. "We should try to get there when it opens. Figure I'll pick you up around eight?"

Cooper nodded. Brent's posture as he backed out the door almost looked like he was fleeing.

"Is he always that high strung?" Cooper's mom asked after Brent was gone.

"I don't know," Cooper answered truthfully. "I just met him this year. Anyway, I should probably get some homework done, since I won't have much time tomorrow."

His mother glanced at the clock. "I need to take over at the shop. Your father isn't feeling very well. It's nothing serious," she added swiftly before Cooper could reply with a deluge of alarmed questions. "He's just a little under the weather and asked me to watch the place for a bit so he could get to the doctor's. There are sandwich fixings in the fridge if you're hungry for lunch."

Cooper nodded. It was about all he could manage, as Ryan's warnings about harming the people near him came to mind. Cooper had been dealing with the shadows all summer, which meant they had been thick inside this house. What kind of shape must his parents be in, living in such conditions?

His father came home an hour later with a prescription for antibiotics, and went straight to bed. Cooper and his mother had leftovers in silence. She looked tired.

Cooper didn't sleep that night. He just simply *didn't*. He told himself he was waiting up for Samantha, but what he was really waiting for was some kind of peace, which he knew he wouldn't find. Instead, the light rain that had been falling much of the day increased until the pounding on the roof seemed to match the thrumming of Cooper's worry.

Around ten-thirty he got up. He managed to catch up with his schoolwork and finish everything that was due on

Monday by midnight. Then he booted up his computer and tried to search the Web for anything on Ryan le Coire or the crazy stuff he had talked about, but there was too much on-line for Cooper to have any idea what might be real or not.

He pulled up a couple of articles on the accident, but couldn't stand to look much past the headlines. He was grateful when he saw lightning through his window, and had an excuse to shut down the computer.

Ryan had asked if the accident was his fault. The answer was yes and no. The weather had been blamed; no citations had been issued. On the other hand, his car *had* been the one in front.

And where was Samantha?

He looked up at the clock, and realized it was a little past one in the morning. He saw that hour too often.

He hoped Samantha was all right. After what she had said about getting lost last time … what if it hadn't had anything to do with trying to talk to Brent in his dreams?

What if she was truly *dying,* losing her connection to this world until she was actually absolutely *gone?* What if the shadowy scavengers Ryan thought Samantha was leading devoured her before Cooper could convince Ryan to protect her?

Needing something to distract himself, he walked to the kitchen. He had just started rummaging for a snack when he saw a flare of light, too sudden and brief to be passing headlights, out of the corner of his eye. In the dark and rain, it was hard to make out the silhouette of a figure, but the glowing tip of a cigarette was unmistakable.

He put down the box of cereal he had found and opened the door, eliciting a startled cry from his mother, who was standing near enough to the door that the eaves were keeping her mostly dry.

"I thought you quit," he said inanely.

She started to say something, stopped, started and stopped again.

"Picked it back up over the summer?" he guessed, trying to keep judgment out of his voice. And guilt. He had spent most of his elementary school years trying to get her to quit, after learning about the dangers of cigarettes in some class presentation. She had finally given it up when he was a freshman.

"I'm sorry," she said.

He shrugged. How could he blame her for coping in her own way? Maybe the smoke burned away the shadows.

"You're up early," she added. "Or late, I guess."

"You too."

"I don't sleep well lately."

"Me either."

He leaned against the wall next to her. She tried to wave away secondhand smoke, but he just ignored it. The falling rain was heavy enough to leave a fine mist on his face.

"It's good to hear you're seeing friends again," she said. "Have I met Brent before?"

"I don't know," Cooper said. "He was at a couple parties

last year with Delilah. We got to chatting the other day. He had a tough summer, too."

"I'm glad you have someone you can talk to," she said, and it was obvious in her tone that she meant it. She put out the cigarette and they both moved back inside. She went to the junk drawer, and asked, "Want to play a round of Go Fish?"

"Sure." Anything to kill time.

The conversation was stunted at first, but at least they were talking for the first time in a long time. They started on neutral topics like how his classes and her job at the bank were going, but as the night wore on they ended up speaking about the accident, and everything that had happened since.

They talked about the hours she had spent in the hospital, wondering if he would survive, and knowing from the doctors' expressions that none of them thought he would. Without mentioning the way they had transitioned into real life, he told her in halted phrases about his nightmares. Almost more painfully, he finally described how mentally and physically exhausting the early sessions with his physical therapist had been, back in the days when it seemed like recovery might hurt more than it was worth.

He wished he could tell her about Samantha, too, who was always there, saying things like, *"You've got a body. It hurts, but it's yours. Trust me when I say you should be grateful. You might never be a football star again, but that's not all there is to life."*

They both jumped when there was a tentative knock at

the door at almost five in the morning. Cooper went to answer it, and frowned when he saw Brent.

"Brent, it's not even sunrise."

"I was going to walk around to your window, since I figured force of habit might have woken you up by now," Brent said, "but I noticed the light on here."

"What happened to eight?"

"Brent?" Cooper's mother sounded concerned. "Come in. Is something wrong?"

The question made Brent flinch. Cooper took a closer look, and realized Brent's face was pale and his lips were pinched. He was also soaking wet.

"Nothing's wrong," he answered, a little too quickly. Cooper could tell his mother didn't believe a word Brent said, either, but she didn't object when he added, "I'm an early riser. I know Cooper is, too. I figured it might be all right to stop by."

"Come in," Cooper said.

Cooper's mother stepped into the hall for a moment, and came back with a dry towel from the linen closet, which she handed to Brent. He accepted it with a soft thank-you and tried to dry off a little as she said, "I'm going to head to bed. You two boys can talk."

She obviously didn't believe Brent's assurances that nothing was wrong—neither did Cooper—but knew better than to press the issue.

The instant she had closed the door, Brent seemed to collapse. He barely made it into a chair, and then he leaned forward until his forehead was on the table and took deep, shuddering breaths.

"Sorry," he said. "It's raining."

Cooper sat down next to him, confused. "What's going on?"

Brent shook his head. "I don't know. I could sense it though, with the same part of me that hears thoughts, for just a minute, and it was . . ." He put his head back down, and rubbed his temples. "I don't know. The storm kept my mum awake. I needed to go somewhere else. It's raining too hard to go to the woods."

Brent wasn't making any sense, but Cooper wasn't going to question him at that moment. He just asked, "Can I do anything for you?"

Brent shook his head. "Just . . . be quiet a minute."

The request was made in vain—the phone rang at that moment, making Brent wince as Cooper hurried to answer it. It wasn't unusual for Cooper to be up at this hour, but why did everyone else seem to be?

"Hello?"

"Cooper?"

He recognized John's voice, and clutched the phone tighter. No one called at this hour with good news. "What's happened?"

"Delilah's in the hospital."

16

While Brent curled up to nap on the couch, wearing one of Cooper's father's shirts as his own dried on the back of a kitchen chair, Cooper carefully worked his body through the exercises his physical therapist had prescribed. Supposedly, if he did them daily, he would maintain nearly normal functioning.

The fear of ending up off his feet again, however, wasn't what had driven him to be diligent that day. He was waiting for a phone call. He had been waiting for almost three hours. The sun had started to rise, and the rain had let up a little, but still no more word since John's call. All he knew was that Delilah was in critical condition. John hadn't had a lot of details and the hospital hadn't been willing to give many more when Cooper asked. But Cooper was on the list of people who would get a call when anyone learned *anything,* most of all if Delilah was going to be okay and when she could have visitors.

He grabbed his cell phone when he heard ringing, only to find it still dark.

Brent let out a grunt and rolled enough to pull his own phone out of his pocket and answer with a sleepy, "Yo." He yawned. "Hi, Ryan . . . Yeah, I heard. . . . No, I don't know anything you don't know." Brent sat up straighter, the last vestiges of grogginess disappearing from his expression. "I heard *that,* too. What was—"

His eyes widened as Ryan must have answered. Cooper crossed the room, but couldn't make out what Ryan was saying.

Brent nodded as he said, "Yeah, we'll be there."

He clicked the phone shut, and then looked up at Cooper.

"I have good news and bad news," he said. "The good news is, Ryan says Delilah is probably going to be okay. She nearly drowned—no, I guess she *actually* drowned, since the paramedics had to resuscitate her. The bad news . . ." He hesitated. "Ryan says she left his house with Samantha. So, either the force that overpowered Delilah—probably the same one that nearly put me out of commission—*was* Samantha, or it was something else Delilah summoned. In which case Ryan says, and I quote, 'A little fish of a power, like Samantha seems to be, may not have fared well.' "

Cooper had to sit down as he felt himself pale. "I haven't seen Samantha since Ryan's house."

"Ryan recommends we go to the hospital and see if Samantha is with Delilah. He'll meet us there."

"Brent—" How could he even begin to express the way his heart was pounding in his throat at the thought of driving down *that* road . . . the one he had been on months ago . . . to the hospital where he had spent weeks. . . .

Of course, he didn't need to say it out loud.

"You must have been on that highway since the accident."

Cooper shook his head. "I was nearly unconscious from medication when I came home from the hospital, and my physical therapist is local. And . . ." He looked out the window. "This doesn't look like good driving conditions."

"Listen. Delilah and I didn't part on the kind of terms where I'm inclined to go racing to her hospital bedside, and I can't check on Samantha without you," Brent said. "I'm willing to drive you there so you can do both those things, but only if you have the courage to get in the damn car. Otherwise, Ryan will just deal with Samantha as he sees fit."

That was enough to motivate Cooper, even if Delilah's condition hadn't been. Two people he cared about were in danger, one of whom had been at his bedside when he woke from nightmares of hell and had stayed with him as he struggled back from it.

Samantha couldn't be evil.

Once Cooper was determined to go, there was still his mother to convince. She looked like she wanted to lock them both in the house, despite Brent's repeated assurances that he would practically *crawl* down the highway, and Cooper's promise to call when they reached the hospital.

"If the rain gets heavy again, you'll pull over instead of trying to bear it out, right?" she asked Brent.

"We'll pull over and we'll call you to let you know we're delayed," he said for perhaps the fifteenth time.

Cooper and Brent left the instant she nodded, before she could consider changing her mind.

"We'll only be on the highway for fifteen minutes or so," Brent said as he backed out of the driveway. "If you can't handle it on your own, I've got half of my mother's medicine cabinet in the glove box. We can always pass you off at the hospital as grieving and distraught, even if you're drugged out of your mind."

"I'll manage without," Cooper said, looking doubtfully at Brent. The casual offer made Cooper realize that, if it weren't for Brent's telepathy and Cooper's extraordinary circumstances, there would probably be more reasons for their not associating than different schools.

Fear took hold as they approached the highway, where other cars were streaming past at disconcerting speeds despite the weather.

"Breathe," Brent whispered as he checked his blind spot, and merged onto the highway. Cooper pressed his palms to the dashboard, and drew deep breaths, closing his eyes tightly and wishing he could drown out the rapid *whoosh-whoosh-whoosh* of Brent's wipers struggling to keep the windshield clear.

Summer vacation. Delilah's parents had a time-share down Cape, and had offered it to the team for a weekend. With summer jobs starting and some parents' nervousness about sending their kids off even under the strict supervision of Delilah's mother, only a half dozen of them were able to go. Cooper was looking forward to it, despite the dreary weather as the trip began.

"Calm, Cooper," Brent said. "It isn't happening now."
Cooper pulled in another deep, rattling breath.
"This was a bad idea," he said.
"Pills are in the glove box," Brent replied.
He wasn't planning to take any, but Cooper used the offer as an excuse to snoop into Brent's life, and to distract himself from what was going on outside the car—namely, movement, road, water, and other cars. "Why do I get the impression you have a very different life than I'm used to?" he pondered out loud as he looked through the collection of prescription drugs. Brent had said they were from his mother's medicine cabinet, but several bottles had Brent's name on them. "Please tell me you do not take this crap when you're driving."

"I don't even take it when I'm sleeping," Brent answered. "When the telepathy got strong enough to be a problem, and I kept ending up in the hospital, doctors always gave me more migraine prescriptions and sleeping pills. I didn't take them because they only made the voices worse, but Mum kept filling the prescriptions if I didn't and— *Damn it, Cooper, stop it!*"

Cooper wasn't sure what he was doing at that exact moment to cause the outburst. "Stop *what?*"

"Stop ... thinking, asking questions," Brent replied tightly. "All I have to do is hit the brake or swerve a little to give you a heart attack, and I swear to God I will if you keep prying."

The words, coupled with the shout, were nearly enough to cause the threatened reaction on their own.

The gray sky had started to drip the moment Cooper got on the road, a fine drizzle that suggested a damp weekend. Hopefully it would pass. This was Massachusetts, after all; the weather was rarely the same from hour to hour.

"Cooper. *Cooper!*" Brent's words jerked him out of the memory. "I'm sorry. I'm tired, and it takes enough concentration to drive without being swamped by your flashbacks that I say stuff without thinking. I don't like to talk about myself, and I *really* don't like to talk about my family, so do me a favor and keep off that subject."

Cooper nodded. If Brent's mother was as unstable as Brent made her seem, Cooper could understand why Brent didn't want to talk about it. He could also guess why telepathy might come in handy.

"I'm sorry," he said. "I won't ask more about your family, but would you talk about *something*? Please. I'm just trying not to think."

"Well, that's kind of you," Brent replied. He paused a moment, and then said, "How about Delilah? There's an interesting girl for you. Doesn't date jocks. Practices black magic in her spare time. On an unrelated note, she likes to dance naked outside on the new moon."

That image was enough to distract Cooper momentarily from his memories of the accident.

Brent laughed, and then said, "For someone who has never dated her, you have a *remarkably* accurate image of her, down to the tattoo on her left hip."

Cooper felt himself blush, as he stammered some kind of excuse about teams and traveling and parties and occasional lack of privacy. "And you two dated?" He still couldn't picture it.

"Yeah, for a while, but then there were some basic ideological incompatibilities. None of that neo-pagan earthy no-personal-gain stuff for that girl," Brent said. "I'm not sure she fancies the 'harm none' principle, either."

"So she *is* a witch?" Cooper asked. "I thought maybe she was like you or something."

"She doesn't like to be called a witch," Brent answered. "She says that gets her confused with the Wiccans and stuff. She plans to become a registered member of the C.O.S. when she turns eighteen."

"C.O.S?"

"Church of Satan."

"Now I *know* you're messing with me," Cooper said. He leaned back, shaking his head. Brent was probably making stuff up to distract him. Probably.

"The Church of Satan isn't the way it's portrayed in movies, with human sacrifice and killing kittens and that Hollywood crap," Brent explained. "A lot of it has to do with personal power, which I'm fine with. However, they do not believe in being kind to those who have 'wronged' them, so I imagine Delilah might have some choice words to say about me, since I kind of implied she was a sociopathic freak when I broke up with her. I think she expected me to be a whole lot more grateful that she passed my name on to Ryan, and she *didn't* expect him to be more impressed by the abilities I got by accident than he is by the ones she worked on for ... oh, never mind."

Cooper looked up at the road—which was a mistake. He knew this stretch of highway. He had seen it in his dreams so many times. The road crested in a hill, and over the hill—

"Stop the car," he gasped.

Brent responded promptly, putting on his hazards, checking for other cars and easing onto the shoulder as quickly as he safely could.

Cooper nearly fell out the passenger-side door, while Brent waited in the car. Leaning over the guardrail, he tried to pull in enough air to keep from passing out as the rain soaked through his clothes. He had nearly succeeded before he lifted his eyes and saw the two white crosses.

He scanned the area, taking in the dents in the guardrails, his mind seeing another day ... and suddenly all the memories came flooding back.

He had tried to slow down, seeing the thick, white fog, but he knew there were people close behind him, and that braking too suddenly on the highway was as dangerous as going too fast. He was riding the brake when he barely saw the flash of movement and color out of his peripheral vision.

He put a hand on the guardrail, in the exact spot the girl had been.

Without slowing, she set one foot on the metal rail and vaulted onto the road.

She landed in front of him, and only then did she turn and seem to see him. Her eyes widened and her mouth opened. He jammed the brake pedal into the floor mat, but she was barely an arm's length away, and nothing could stop the series of collisions that followed.

An enormous crash, and then he was airborne. Shattering glass, and impact.

Had Samantha been the one who leaped in front of his car that day? But there had been no mention of a girl being killed in the crash. Cooper had checked. Unless Ryan was right, and she had never been alive in the first place. In which case the real question was: had she known what she was doing, and the damage she would cause?

10

Delilah felt like she was drowning, not in rain, but in fire. The world seemed to be ablaze. She couldn't make sense of it. She wished she was dreaming. If she had been, she could have woken herself. But this was more like wandering, lost.

She remembered the way the skies had split while she tried to figure out how to link to Samantha. The rain that had fallen around her had been so thick she couldn't draw air into her lungs. With every breath, she had inhaled more water. But this was something different, someone else's memory of another time and place.

She drew a breath, but it was a futile one. Her lungs were scorched by smoke and heat. She struggled forward despite every survival instinct telling her to run, because she could hear screaming.

Delilah knew she wasn't some helpless child. She was a sorcerer.

I think, therefore I am, she pondered. If she still existed, then she was still alive, and she did not have to linger this way. And if she was alive, then she could learn.

Instead of struggling toward consciousness, she reached for the memory of fire. She had tried to bind a water elemental, and had found a vision of flames and . . . something. Pain, yes, but more than that.

She woke in the hospital with a shudder and found herself shouting, "Leave me alone!"

Her eyes were barely open before Ryan began the lecture she had anticipated. "What did you think you were *doing?*" he demanded, only to answer his own question before she could draw a breath into her aching lungs. "No, I know what you thought you were doing. You thought you were being clever, and bold."

"No less so than Arabella le Coire once was," she managed to gasp out. Ryan's ancestor had bound herself to an earth elemental and set herself up as lady of a great manor—the same manor where she had been imprisoned, awaiting death for heresy and witchcraft before then. Hundreds of years later, the le Coire family still had immense power, all from that ancient bargain.

"One would think you might have learned *something* after you were nearly devoured by the scavengers when you were twelve, but no! I hoped that, sometime in the three years you've worked with *me*, I would have imparted some actual wisdom. And I *prayed* you would learn when you sent three other people into howling madness with that trick you pulled last spring—but by then I was a little less optimistic. Now this!"

He stood up and began to pace. Delilah shut her eyes again, exhausted.

"Do you even know whose flesh you're wearing?" he demanded.

"What?"

That got her attention. She tried to sit up, only to have pain ricochet through her body.

"Her name was Margaret," Ryan said. "The last time I spoke to her was in May. She told me she had found a way to bind one of the elemental powers. I can only assume it was based in fire, since the next thing I heard was that her entire family was lost in a pyre so hot it melted the steel frame of the car in the driveway. She managed to make it out of the house. Some hikers found her in the forest two weeks later, battered and savaged by animals. She wouldn't have survived physically if she hadn't snagged *some* power from her elemental, but since her mind is completely gone, the fact that her heart is still beating doesn't make much of a difference."

Delilah tried to lift her head to look at herself, but would not have succeeded if Ryan hadn't cranked the bed up. Even covered by a sheet, she could still tell that this thin and wiry body was not her own. She struggled to lift her arm, and saw that her nails had the remnants of chipped, mauve nail polish on them. When she touched her head, she found dark hair barely long enough for her to pull it forward to look at it.

"Why am I here?" she asked Ryan.

"Your exposure to Cooper probably made you vulnerable," he answered. "When your body was stressed, you lost control of your tie to it. You're lucky you were able to protect yourself long enough to find another vessel to keep you alive, since I imagine it would have been impossible to return to your normal form while it was still on the verge of death. I had a hard time purging the extra power from you long enough to clear the water out of your—oh, there they are. Cooper! Brent!"

She managed to turn her head enough to see the guys respond to Ryan's call. Both were dripping wet, and Cooper was as pale as the sheet covering Margaret's body.

"They said Delilah is in room—"

"Delilah's right here for the moment," Ryan interrupted. "Cooper, would you check Delilah's room to see if Samantha is there?"

"Wait," Delilah objected. "What *exactly* do you mean by that?" It was one thing for her to be accidentally and temporarily in someone else's body. It was another if the power she had attempted to harness had helped itself to *her* body.

"Just check, Cooper," Ryan said. "Brent, tell the nurse on duty that Margaret is conscious."

Brent and Cooper exchanged confused glances, but then hastened to obey the command. Delilah wasn't surprised. Brent always did anything Ryan ordered, most of the time without bothering to even ask why.

She hated to ask Ryan for anything, especially given how often she ended up doing so, but she swallowed her pride. "Can you help me stand?"

"No."

"Just help me up already," she grumbled. "I want to see my own body, and make sure it's all right."

"Given this body has been unconscious for months, I'm not even going to let you sit up completely until a medical professional assures me it's safe. After that, we'll need a wheelchair. Or have you not tried to move your legs yet?"

She hadn't. In fact, she hadn't even thought of them. The rest of her body was in pain, so her legs had been the least of her worries. Once he had pointed it out, though, she realized the obvious. "I can't feel them."

"Margaret's back is broken," Ryan answered. "The doctors have told me that it's a low break, so it doesn't affect any major systems, but the paralysis of her legs is probably total."

Cooper returned, and reported, "Samantha isn't there, and Delilah is still unconscious. They've got her on some kind of breathing thing. So, *who* is this?"

Before Ryan could answer, Brent returned with the nurse, who had a slightly dazed look in her eyes. Ryan or Brent or both of them had probably done a number on her mind, convincing her to let them all in here outside visiting hours.

The nurse checked Delilah's ... no, *Margaret's* vitals. Delilah refused to think of this body as herself. She was borrowing it for a little while. That was all.

"When can you get me out of here?" she asked Ryan. "And back in my own body?"

Ryan nodded, though slowly. "Cooper should be able to knock you out of this body. I can keep the shadows at bay so you are not damaged without your flesh. With your own power to guide you, you should be able to reinhabit your own body without trouble now that it is no longer drowning."

Cooper seemed less calm. "Wait, I can *what*? Who says I can do this intentionally?"

"You were going to come back to study with me, weren't you?" Ryan asked. "Consider this your first lesson."

"I'm not entirely comfortable with having my 'first lesson' involve another person," Cooper said.

Delilah found herself smiling, impressed to see Cooper, who she had always thought of as something of a teddy bear, standing up to Ryan. He did so in his own mellow way, but it was still more than she had ever seen Brent do.

At that moment, for example, Brent was leaning against the far wall with his eyes closed. She could recognize the tension between his brows as a sign of one of his ever-present headaches.

"It's all right, Cooper," she assured him. "Sometimes you have to risk a little to learn a little."

Cooper looked like he was going to continue to argue, but before he could, a flicker of shadow caused them all to turn toward the other side of the room. Samantha's colorful form looked like crystal as the afternoon sun streamed through it. There were tears on her face.

"I didn't mean it!" she cried. "I didn't know what was going on. I got scared! I just—I mean, I—" She broke off as she noticed the figure on the hospital bed, and her face took on an expression of cold horror.

"Samantha. Nice of you to join us," Ryan said. He looked wary, but to his credit, he stepped between the elemental and the three humans without hesitating. "I gather you have benefited from Delilah's experiments, since the four of us can all see you clearly now. Delilah didn't fare quite so well, but she'll be fine in a few minutes. Cooper, is that the face she has always had to you?"

Cooper nodded, and pushed past Ryan, heedless of any danger the elemental might represent. "Samantha, are you . . ." She lifted a hand as if to grasp his, but her hand passed through his. They both frowned. "I believe you that it wasn't your fault."

"Then you're the only one in this room who does," Ryan muttered under his breath.

"What happened to the person who was in this body?" Cooper asked, looking at Delilah.

Ryan swallowed tightly, and for a brief moment, Delilah thought he might actually display a hint of emotion. His words, however, were blunt. "She's gone. Once Delilah's essence is returned to its rightful place, this body will once again be inert. Margaret has no blood relations left, so her guardianship has fallen to my family, since we were her mentors. I have been pursuing the process of having her body taken off life support."

"There's no possibility of her recovering, even with your magic?" Cooper asked.

Ryan shook his head, though he was looking at Samantha, who had crept toward the bed. Having her so near made Delilah nervous. She might have looked like a pretty teenage girl, but the expression in her eyes as she stared at Delilah was very far away, and not entirely human.

"Then..." Cooper drew a deep breath. "Is there... I mean, this sounds horrible to even ask, but if she's really gone and there's nothing else..." He trailed off, and looked to Ryan and Brent for help, but neither offered it. Cooper managed at last to put the words together. "You thought Samantha might have been in Delilah's body, right? That means you think she *could* do something like that. What about this body? Once Delilah is back in her own, could this one maybe make it possible for Samantha to be alive?" He winced. "I know this girl was a friend of yours or something, but—"

"Samantha's an elemental," Delilah said. "She doesn't need to use another body to have form. She should be able to create one, once she is bound to a mortal being."

"She obviously isn't powerful enough to maintain that

kind of connection, or she would have done it already,"
Ryan said. "Using another's form is probably the only op-
tion she has, and it is *not* acceptable. Delilah, if you knew
Margaret, you would realize—"

"Stop talking like I'm not here!" Samantha's shriek made the
panes of the windows rattle. "I don't want that . . . that
thing!" She reached forward, and Delilah tensed for a blow,
but she could not have expected the sensations that followed.

Samantha didn't hit Margaret's body; she actually hit
Delilah. Delilah felt herself shoved outward and up-
ward. Disoriented, and fighting to regain some kind
of control, she saw chaos break out. Samantha hit Ryan
before he had any chance to defend himself, and as he
crumpled, Samantha turned to the body on the hospital
bed. Cooper, Brent, and Samantha were all shouting, the
words overlapping each other but sounding muffled. All
Delilah could tell was that Samantha had gone mad and
was determined to kill the figure on the bed.

"You don't have to!" Cooper shouted. "If you don't want
to—"

"She shouldn't *be* here!" Samantha wailed. "She should
be dead. She shouldn't have lived!"

To Delilah's surprise, Brent stepped forward, taking
charge of the situation. He gripped Cooper's bare arm
with one hand, and then reached toward Samantha's form
with his other hand.

The shock waves that followed sent Delilah tumbling

backward into darkness . . . and then again into memories of fire.

Tears snapped and sizzled as they fell into the flames. What had she done?

"Tell me where you are!" she shouted. She could hear the screaming, but she couldn't find the source. "Please!"

The fire was starting to get too hot, and the power she had summoned was starting to fade in the face of her despair.

Delilah woke with a gasp, her body spasming as her lungs struggled to eject phantom water and smoke. *Her* lungs; *her* body. She was still in the hospital, but she was in her own skin. Now, what about everyone else?

✂2✂

Cooper woke on a hospital bed, with his mother sitting pale-faced beside him. "How long have I been out?" he asked.

"Only a few hours, and you've just been sleeping naturally for most of it. Long enough for them to check your wallet and call me. Thank God the hospital had the sense to tell me you were all right before they told me you fainted," his mother said, gripping his hand tightly enough that he winced. "They ran some drug tests, but those came back clean, of course. They've scheduled you for a CAT scan and an MRI to make sure nothing's wrong. Your father wanted to be here, but the doctors said he needs to be on antibiotics for twenty-four hours before he's out and about."

Cooper nodded, the small movement causing his head to spin as he tried to piece together his jumbled memories of what had happened. Samantha had gone berserk. Cooper's idiotic suggestion had sent her into a frenzy far beyond anything he could have predicted. Then Brent... well, he wasn't sure what Brent had done.

"How is Brent?"

"I take it the two of you had stopped in to visit with a cousin of his? I heard him telling doctors he hasn't eaten in a while, and I gather he fainted, too. The doctors think your reaction may have been a result of the combined stress of Delilah's condition, and your friend's sudden collapse. Delilah is awake, by the way. They say she's going to be fine."

Well, that was something, at least. He just wasn't quite sure what it all meant.

Shouting suddenly began across the hall, audible through the closed door.

"How dare you do this to me?" a woman shrieked. "Don't you think I have better things to do than hike all the way here to pick up after you? Don't you ever think about anyone but yourself?"

Cooper's mother's eyes went wide, and she stood up, seeming indignant.

"And they tell me they're doing drug tests! Drugs! You've been stealing from the medicine cabinet, I'm sure of it. Don't you know what I go through, when I get a call from the hospital, telling me my son has taken an overdose and passed out?"

"Oh, that's *it,*" Cooper's mother said, pushing herself up

and crossing the room in angry strides. "Excuse me," he heard her say as she approached the woman who had to be Brent's mother. "But do you *really* think that right here and now is the best time to yell at your son?"

"How *dare* you tell me how to speak to my own child?"

"First off, there has been *no* indication of drugs, so that's quite an accusation," she said. "Second, Brent probably passed out due to the fact he hasn't *eaten* a decent *meal* in days. Third, he's in the *hospital,* visiting his very ill friend, and obviously distressed. Far be it from me to tell someone else how to raise her child but you are out of line."

A nurse interrupted before the argument could escalate much further. "Ladies, why don't you come downstairs with me, and we'll get some coffee?" the nurse suggested. "This kind of disruption isn't good for any of the patients."

Cooper was sure his mother only agreed because she knew it was the best way to convince Brent's mother to stop yelling at Brent.

As soon as the three of them were gone, Brent emerged. He was moving with a strange deliberateness, and seemed a little unsteady on his feet as he crossed Cooper's room.

"That was your mom?" Cooper asked.

Brent winced. "Apparently." He shook his head. "The doctors say I'm good to go, at least. I guess they want to keep you overnight for observation?"

"That's what I've been told," Cooper said. "I gather they

want to make sure my brain's not about to explode from some damage left from the accident. What did you do back there, with Samantha?"

Brent looked away. "I'm not even sure. I guess it was instinct. You're okay though, right?" Brent tilted his head, making eye contact for the first time since he walked in. There was something unsettling about his expression as he put a hand on Cooper's arm. "Can you sit up?"

Cooper hadn't even noticed he was still lying down. He was more out of it than he thought.

He pushed himself into an upright position, only to then have to lean forward as a second wave of vertigo hit. Black spots danced in his vision. Brent kept him from falling forward off the bed by sitting next to him and looping an arm across Cooper's shoulders.

Cooper drew a couple of deep breaths, until the world stopped rocking beneath him.

"How are Ryan and Delilah?" he asked, wondering how Brent was doing so much better than he was.

"Haven't seen them," Brent replied. "The nurses didn't want me to stand up at first, just kept insisting on feeding me and stuff to get my blood pressure back up. Then that woman—my mom, I mean—came in."

"What about—" Cooper stopped, distracted, when he realized Brent still had an arm over his shoulders. Had he always been this touchy-feely?

"What about what?" Brent asked.

"Samantha," he managed to say. "Do you know what

happened to her?" Before Brent could actually respond, though, the cuddling got to be a little much for him, so he just blurted out, "Are you hitting on me?"

"What?" Brent blinked with surprise.

Cooper deliberately lifted Brent's arm off his shoulders.

"Oh," Brent said. But instead of moving away, he came closer, and leaned over Cooper as if to kiss him before Cooper shoved him.

"Back off!" Cooper pushed himself to his feet and took a slightly unsteady step away. This could explain why Brent and Delilah hadn't worked out. "You've been really cool the last few days, and I appreciate the help you've given me, and I'm happy to have you as a friend. But I don't swing that way. Got it?"

Brent started laughing. He put his hands on his hips and shook his head.

"Cooper . . ." He took a breath, obviously struggling not to keep laughing. Eventually he managed to say. "You're really not very bright all the time, are you? Maybe I should come back when you're a little more together," he said.

"Yeah, you do that," Cooper said. "Come back *later*." When the world was back to normal, at least.

"I thought you would be cool with this," Brent said, slinking forward with a half smile and another chuckle. "You'll laugh when you get over the surprise."

"Ha-ha," Cooper said flatly. "Now go away."

Brent shook his head and turned, but there was something familiar about the movement that made Cooper frown. When Brent walked back toward the door—with a bit of a huffy flounce in his step—Cooper said, "Wait."

"Make up your mind," Brent said with a smile.

"I . . ." He stared at Brent, examining the way he was standing, half turned with one hand on his hip and his head just slightly tilted with teasing curiosity. He asked quietly, "Samantha?"

He recognized her giggle now, despite its deeper tone and the form it accompanied. "I wondered how long it would take you to figure it out." She moved closer this time, her posture still flirtatious, and more obviously feminine now that he realized what was going on.

She reached for him again, and he leaped back with a yelp only partially caused by the pain that shot down his hip from the sudden tense movement.

"Oh, come on," she said. "It's not like I'm *actually* a guy."

"No, that would be far more okay," Cooper retorted hotly. "I'd still say no, but . . . God, Samantha, what the *hell*? You're a chick in a dude, who's hitting on me, which is creepy enough. But that's not just some random body. It's taken already."

"It's not like I did this intentionally," she protested. "I wouldn't know how to undo it if I wanted to."

Refusing to get distracted, Cooper asked, "Samantha— should I even call you that? *Where is Brent?* I haven't seen him, the way I used to be able to see you. Is he okay?"

Samantha sighed and flipped her hair, though it really wasn't long enough for the gesture.

"Don't know, don't care," she said. "I'm sure he's fine wherever he is. I managed it for months."

"Samantha—"

"Cooper," she crooned. She caught his hand, and held on to it tightly. "Do you understand what it's like, to have a body? To be able to touch you—or anything, really," she said. "They gave me applesauce when I woke up, and just a simple thing like that was incredible. I didn't do this on purpose. I don't know what you and Brent were doing or tried to do, just that I woke up like this. But I won't regret it. I *can't* regret it. I'm *alive*."

She kissed his cheek and then gave a gentle push, sending him stumbling toward the hospital bed.

"I'll keep in touch," she said, before the air shuddered again. This time Cooper didn't think it was his head that was spinning.

When he managed to look up again, Samantha was gone.

What next? Cooper hoped Ryan or Delilah would be able to help, but he remembered how easily Samantha had knocked Ryan down at the start of her hysterical attack on Margaret's body. Would Cooper find Ryan in another room around here, unconscious or worse?

More importantly, would he find Brent at all?

There was one place Cooper could check for Brent, the only place he could imagine his being able to go. If Brent was there, things were going to be . . . kind of funny, actually.

21

Brent wasn't laughing. He was very far from laughing.

The fight with Samantha was hazy in his memory. All he really remembered was trying to use some combination of his telepathy and Cooper's power over spirits to try to push Samantha away before she hurt someone. He thought he had succeded, but the next thing he knew, he was flying through darkness.

In the world between worlds lay the shadowy demons of which Ryan had spoken. They had reached for him and ripped at him, and all he could do was flee. He tried to find his own body. . . .

Instead he had woken up here in a hospital bed.

The fact that he was in a girl's body—even a paralyzed, weakened body—was a very minor inconvenience, compared to the other facts of the matter.

He felt deaf. The ability to read thoughts was something he had cursed many times, but it was a sense he had grown used to. Now, the entire world seemed flat and silent. When he was alone, not speaking to anyone or answering doctors' and nurses' questions, the silence was overpowering. He felt like he could hear those *creatures* in the darkness, beneath the empty air, and it made his heart race. When he did manage to drift off, he had nightmares in which he was lost in a fiery hell, searching for someone very important to him.

A doctor was supposed to be coming later to tell him the details of his condition, but he already knew that there was simply no feeling below his waist, and that was a whole lot better than how he felt above it. He could move his arms, but doing so hurt, and his muscles trembled when he tried. One of the nurses had told him that a lot of the pain and weakness was not a result of injury, but of being bed-bound for months. Physical therapy would help him regain full use of his upper body.

Or, of *her* upper body—the one he was trapped in at the moment.

He hoped it wouldn't be his very long. Ryan hadn't been too concerned when this happened to Delilah, but Ryan hadn't stopped in yet.

He let out a frustrated noise, and hit the nurse call button. Someone appeared almost immediately to ask what was wrong.

He felt stupid even asking, but the silence was driving him insane.

"Is there a radio or television or something, somewhere?" he asked. "It's so quiet in here."

She nodded, with a smile, and patted his hand. "I'll see what I can get for you."

Brent had never been so glad to see anyone as he was to see Cooper when he came in the room halfway through some strange anime cartoon show Brent had put on for noise but hadn't been able to follow. Cooper paused in the doorway awkwardly for a moment before asking, "Brent?"

"Yeah," he confirmed.

Cooper's body sagged and he leaned back against the wall with a relieved sigh. "With everything Ryan said about people not being able to survive without their bodies, I was worried you might be—"

"Should I take that to mean you've seen where the rest of me got to?" Brent interrupted.

Cooper nodded and looked so guilty Brent didn't need telepathy to figure out why.

"Samantha," Brent guessed. He closed his eyes, exhausted from the effort of talking. He had heard his mother yelling at "him," and so had known his body was up and around, but he had been in and out of consciousness too much since then to track where he had gone. "Where's Ryan? Is he hurt?"

"I don't know. I came here first, after I realized what had happened. Want me to look for him?"

"Don't bother." Delilah's voice from the doorway

sounded hoarse. At least *she* ended up in the right place. "He's pissed at us all." Brent opened his eyes to find Delilah leaning in the doorway, holding up a gift-shop card with a teddy bear on the front. She read from the inside: " 'When the three of you stop acting like children and make up your minds as to what you want, call me. Until then, clean up your own mess.' He's grumpy that Samantha got the best of him."

"He's 'grumpy' that you nearly got yourself killed again," Brent replied.

"Do you spend *all* your life kissing le Coire's—"

"Enough!" Cooper snapped, stepping between them. "Ryan has a right to be upset. Beyond anything we've done intentionally, you two have ended up squatting in a body that used to belong to someone he *knows*, remember? Someone who apparently died pretty horribly, because she messed up while using powers Ryan was supposed to help her with. I was an idiot to suggest what I did. Apparently even Samantha agrees. And now I don't know what to do or what to think about her—" He broke off and had to draw a deep breath. "But I think it's obvious that Brent has a right to his own body. I get that you two had a bad breakup, but can we maybe focus for just a minute on what's important?"

Brent nodded. Unfortunately, he wasn't the one who needed to agree, since Delilah was the only one in the room who had any idea how to handle elementals or the shadow-scavengers.

Delilah was staring at Cooper with a lazy, contented smile that seemed ill-suited to the situation. "Cooper Blake grows a spine," she said. "I'll help—or try to—"

"Why?" Brent interrupted, suspicious.

"It couldn't be out of the goodness of my heart?" she replied sweetly, batting her eyelashes. He didn't deign to respond, and at last she glared at him instead. "I'm not one of le Coire's lapdogs, but I respect him. He's going to blame me for this mess, as usual. I don't want him to have to clean it up."

Brent hadn't thought that Delilah worried about anyone's opinion.

Then again, she was captain of the cheerleading squad, house director for the drama department, and practiced sorcery in her spare time. That drive for success had to come from somewhere.

"Anyway," she said, "I'm pretty sure I can summon Samantha. According to Ryan she's not very strong, and I think she'll be even weaker now that she's condensed herself in order to occupy a relatively normal human body—no offense, Brent. That's kind of like saying she's a relatively weak hurricane, though. I can get her here, but I'm not going to be able to control her if she fights us."

"Is it just me, or did she react a little too strongly to the idea of taking Margaret's body?" Brent asked, recalling the strange scene.

"Maybe she didn't like the idea of going from an immortal power to a wheelchair," Delilah suggested.

Cooper shook his head. "Do you know how many times she told me over the last few months that all she wanted was to be *alive*? When I first woke up, the doctors weren't sure if I would ever be able to walk. It was Samantha who convinced me that my life wasn't any less valid just because I couldn't do everything I used to be able to do. I don't think the possibility of a disability would have kept her from accepting a chance to live, and even if it did, that wouldn't explain how strongly she reacted."

"Maybe your connection to Samantha *is* actually kind of coincidental." Delilah paced the room as she spoke. "Does anyone remember a fire around here? Ryan said a whole family was killed. I don't remember it, but I don't watch the news a lot."

Cooper sat heavily in one of the guest chairs next to the bed. "Yeah, it was all over the television, just a few days be-fore ... before the accident. My mom was pretty freaked out. She went around checking smoke detectors and bought a second fire extinguisher and a fire ladder for my room. You don't think Samantha *caused* the fire, do you? And killed all those people?"

"I think we have a sorcerer named Margaret, who was trying to summon an elemental, but burned down her house and then was found in bad shape right around the time that Samantha appeared. A water elemental wouldn't have started the fire, but they're drawn to grief and bound in tears. Margaret accidentally slaughtered her entire family. A sorcerer with that much power and that much emotional pain might have been able to create something like Samantha."

Delilah's words made some of the puzzle-pieces fall into place. "Ryan seemed to recognize Samantha when Cooper and I came to his house," Brent said.

Delilah looked straight at him, with the wide-eyed excitement that had attracted him to her in the first place. "Of course!" she exclaimed as if suddenly everything made sense. "When I was in Margaret's body, I picked up on some of her memories. They make sense now. In all the memories I picked up, she was trying to get to someone. She didn't care about saving herself, but she needed to save this other person, who was screaming."

Brent hadn't been able to track Margaret's memories as well as Delilah obviously had, but when Delilah started to describe them, he remembered the nightmares. "Her sister," he said.

"It had to be Samantha," Delilah answered, gripping Brent's hand for a moment before realizing what she was doing and dropping it. "Not *our* Samantha. Her Samantha, her sister."

"Didn't we already establish a while ago that Samantha *isn't* a ghost?" Cooper asked.

"She's *not*," Delilah answered excitedly. "She *is* an elemental, but she's shaped the way Margaret made her. Margaret couldn't control the fire elemental she tried to summon, but she would have raised so much power to do so that when things went wrong, a water elemental was attracted to the chaos. Margaret named it, so it took the personality and form of the being she *wanted* to see. It all makes sense!"

Brent and Cooper exchanged a glance. Cooper's dazed expression said he was equally confused. Brent knew without a doubt that he was right about Margaret's relationship with Samantha, but he had never understood sorcery and elemental powers. He had to trust that Delilah knew what she was talking about.

One thing still didn't make sense. "But if we're right, why did Samantha try to kill her sister?" Brent asked. "Twice."

"Guilt," Cooper suggested. "Our Samantha isn't the real girl, right?" He looked at Delilah, who nodded. "She's what Margaret created. Margaret had to blame herself for her sister's death. That guilt—self-hatred even, I'd guess—could have been part of what she put into the Samantha we saw."

"If we know all that, then now what?" Brent asked. "Samantha's some kind of baby elemental impersonating a teenage girl. Do we—"

"Not impersonating," Delilah interrupted. "The elementals are just raw power on their own. They have no memories or senses of *self* until mortal minds create them. What Margaret gave her is all Samantha knows."

"Ha!" Cooper shouted a little too triumphantly. "Sorry," he mumbled. "But I was right. She's *not* evil."

"She walked off with my body," Brent pointed out.

"She'll give it back," Cooper said confidently. "If she *is* the girl that I've known for months—and according to Delilah, she is—then she doesn't mean to hurt anyone. As soon as we find her, I'm sure I can convince her to do what's right."

This time it was Brent's and Delilah's turn to exchange a skeptical look. But what else could they do?

"I'll summon her," Delilah said with a shrug.

I hope you're right, Brent thought, still not entirely convinced. He might not understand sorcery, but he had picked up enough hints over the last few days to know that if Samantha wasn't on their side, she was more than powerful enough to drown them all.

❧22❧

Two hours later, Cooper watched as Delilah spoke to a nurse in low, even tones. She had already convinced Cooper's mother to go home and take care of his sick father. Now, she had a hand on the nurse's shoulder. Their eyes were linked, and there was sweat on Delilah's brow.

"So you see, it's very important that we're not interrupted," Delilah said.

The nurse nodded. "I will speak to the others on the floor."

"Good," Delilah said with a nod, finally breaking eye contact. "Thank you, nurse. We really appreciate this."

"Well. Religious observances are important," the nurse mumbled, as if struggling to recall what she had just been doing.

"Yes. Thank you." Delilah patted her hand, and as the

nurse went about her way, Cooper followed Delilah back into Margaret's room. "I convinced her that we're doing a Native American healing ritual that is very important to Brent culturally and religiously and we must not be interrupted."

Curious, Cooper said, "I assume you did a little more than *talk* to her, since she didn't even question the fact that no one in this room looks remotely Native American."

"I have some talents." Delilah ducked her head before saying with obvious pride, "You should see what Ryan can do. I have to work with what people are already thinking and inclined to do. You heard the nurse ask if we were going to be lighting candles or incense? If I had said yes, we probably would have had a problem. Ryan could have convinced her to light *herself* on fire, without even needing to say it out loud. And Brent—"

"Keep me out of this," Brent interrupted.

Delilah stuck out her tongue at him, though the expression was playful this time, and less hostile than before. "Modesty is not a trait I admire."

" 'Creepy' is not a trait *I* admire," Brent replied. "And thought control falls in the realm of creepy in my book. I only let Ryan teach me what I could do so I wouldn't do it accidentally."

Cooper resisted the impulse to take a step away from both of them. "So, we've got the room to ourselves," he said. "What now?"

"Now . . . now," Delilah said with a shaky breath, "I try

to remember that, if something goes wrong, at least I'm already in a hospital."

Cooper felt alarmed and shamed as he asked, "How dangerous is this for you?" He understood that they needed Delilah's help to get Brent back where he should be, but as far as he knew, Delilah didn't need *them* for anything. Yet she was still here.

Delilah looked nervous, as she crossed her legs to sit on the hospital floor, but she flashed a bold grin as she said, "Like I told you earlier, Coop, sometimes this work requires a little risk. People without the guts to face that shouldn't get into sorcery."

She closed her eyes, and tossed her hair back as she lifted her chin rather than bowing her head.

Cooper shifted his weight from foot to foot, wondering what was supposed to happen, and if he should be doing anything in particular. Delilah had promised the nurse that there would be no incense or candles or loud noises that might disturb other patients, but Cooper had still expected a little ritual and pizzazz.

After a minute, he whispered to Brent, "Has she started?"

Brent laughed out loud, though the raspy sound quickly turned to a cough. "I don't do this stuff, remember?" he asked. "I'd feel a lot better if I had any clue what was happening, or if it were just about anyone but Delilah we had to rely on."

"If you two would just be quiet ...," Delilah started to say, but trailed off.

Cooper sat back down.

The first indication that *anything* was happening was the sweat that seemed to gather on his skin despite the steady hum of the air conditioner. The room didn't get hot exactly, but rather stifling and muggy. He shivered.

Twenty minutes passed without anyone speaking or moving. The air continued to thicken, until condensation built up on all the surfaces. Drops ran down the inside of the windowpanes. It was so foggy Cooper had to move his chair inward to keep both Brent and Delilah in sight. He hoped that whatever Delilah had done to the nurse would keep anyone else from responding to the change in atmospheric conditions.

He realized Delilah's lips were moving, as if she were speaking without sound, and it was becoming harder and harder to breathe. Suddenly the room seemed to constrict. He dropped his head, trying to pull air into his lungs as the edges of his sight turned from white fog to black mist. He tried to make it to the door, to get out and somehow break the effect, but succeeded only in falling to his knees on the floor.

Thank God, he thought, as the door opened with a *bang*.

The sound was followed by Samantha's petulant accent, coming from Brent's body, as she said, "I have Brent's *phone!* Did it not occur to anyone to *call* me?"

The fog started to clear, and Cooper drew in deep, gasping breaths. Ryan helped him to his feet.

"Would you have come?" Delilah asked. She sounded winded, but not as badly as Cooper.

Samantha hesitated, before saying, "Maybe."

"What are you doing here?" Brent said, looking up at Ryan.

"Samantha needed a ride," Ryan replied nonchalantly.

Brent's voice was choked as he demanded, "What did you do to my *car*?"

"Your *mother* took the keys!" Samantha shouted back. "I didn't know how to stop her without hurting her."

Cooper's head had finally stopped spinning, and the air had returned to normal, when a nurse walked by and looked into the room. "What is going on—"

"We're fine," Ryan, Samantha and Delilah answered in unison. The nurse literally rocked back on her heels before nodding, her gaze unfocused, and continued down the hall.

Ryan closed the door.

"Did you even have a plan for what you were going to do next?" Ryan asked.

He looked exhausted, which made Cooper pause. Ryan acted so much older then the rest of them, but it occurred to Cooper that he was probably young enough to still be in college. He had the type of responsibility Cooper hoped to avoid for a long time.

Delilah and Brent both hesitated, Delilah visibly bristling at the scorn in Ryan's voice.

Cooper faced Samantha. "Brent and Delilah think they've figured out who you are."

"You mean *what*," she said bitterly.

He shook his head. "No, I mean *who*. I mean, yes, I guess

we've all figured out that you're not human, and that you never really were. That you used to be some kind of massive, formless power. But you're more than that. You're . . ." He looked from Samantha to the figure on the bed. "I know you don't have a lot of memories, but I also know you sometimes *do* remember things once you see them. Look at her, Samantha. Do you recognize her at all?"

Samantha stared at Margaret's body. Brent's hazel eyes widened, and then flashed silver, but then Samantha shook her head. "Not . . . really. It's like I almost remember."

"I don't understand it all," Cooper admitted, "but she created you in the image of someone she cared about a great deal. She's the one who made you Samantha."

"If you're willing," Delilah said cautiously, "the rest of her memories, and the memories she would have given you, are still locked in her flesh. I know you're probably very angry with her. You probably don't even really understand why. But if you give Brent back his body, and use Margaret's instead, then it will help you be—"

"Excuse me?" Ryan protested. "It was bad enough when Cooper suggested it, but did I just hear you offer up someone *else's* body to—"

"To *Samantha!*" Delilah interrupted, shouting over Ryan. "I was only in her memories for a short while, but I can tell you, Margaret would have given *everything* to save her sister. If you worked with her, you must know how close they were."

"This isn't Samantha," Ryan insisted. "It looks like Samantha, but it's—"

"And this isn't Margaret. It's a shell. It's a body. And Samantha is all that's left of either sister."

"What if I don't want to go anywhere?" Samantha argued. "I like *this* body. It's loud, but if Brent could learn to control that, so can I."

"Samantha." Cooper stepped toward her, and took her hands, trying to get his mind past who she *looked* like and remember who she was. "We've spent most of the past few months together. You've gotten me through hard times. And no matter what anyone says, I know you're a good person. You're giddy to have a body at all right now, but you have to remember that this one isn't *yours*. You've stolen it from someone else. Someone who was doing everything he could to help us."

Samantha chewed on her lower lip. "What if I don't *want* Margaret's memories?"

"Remember how scared I was?" Cooper asked, still holding Samantha's hands. "You helped me get through everything that happened to me. We'll get you through this now."

"Can't I just keep this body for a little while?" Samantha asked. "So I can, I don't know, get used to having a body before I need to deal with *her*? I want to go out dancing. I want to . . . God, I want to run *away*. I've never been as scared as I am when I look at her, and I don't even know why."

"The longer you're in Brent's body, the more of a permanent effect you might have on it," Delilah said. "You don't realize how much power you possess, Samantha. You limit yourself by claiming flesh at all." Ryan cleared his throat, and Delilah snapped, "What? It's true!"

"I don't want power," Samantha said flatly. "I know Ryan's afraid of what I might do if I actually decide to be what I am, but I don't want to be some kind of immortal *thing*. I just want to be . . . alive, a person." She drew a breath. "Isn't there another choice?"

"You're not powerful enough to create your own body," Ryan said with a sigh. "And your consciousness as Samantha is too restricted to allow it to survive long without a mortal form."

"Then . . . then I guess there's no choice." With a lopsided smile, Samantha said, "Brent, I guess we're swapping. And . . . I'm sorry. I never meant to hurt you."

"I'll leave you crazy kids to your games," Ryan said, turning away.

"You're not going to help?" Delilah asked.

"I'm going to cast a secondary circle outside this room, to keep the hospital staff and scavengers out, and any other power inside. If you screw up, I won't let it hurt anyone else in the building. That's my role in this. You're all too old for me to hold your hands. Delilah . . ." Ryan paused, and shook his head. "Be careful."

He closed the door softly behind him.

❧ 23 ❧

Cooper could taste his anxiety as Delilah, Brent and Samantha looked at him hopefully.

"This is all you, Coop," Delilah said. "The only thing I can do is try to temper Samantha's power so it doesn't go crazy again."

"I got scared before," Samantha said. "In the woods. I got so scared."

"I guess you've got an excuse for it," Delilah said grudgingly. "The last time anyone around you tried to work with an elemental, you kind of died in a raging inferno. I'm going to have to ask you to try *very* hard to stay calm this time."

"I feel better about this already," Brent said dryly.

"Remind me what I'm supposed to be doing again?" Cooper asked. "You know I've only ever done this body-swap thing accidentally, right?"

"Yes?" Delilah said slowly, and looked at Brent. "I know with my kind of power, a lot of it is just thinking through what I want to happen, and kind of *willing* it."

" 'Focused attention' is what Ryan calls it," Brent said. Despite the barbs Delilah and Brent kept throwing at each other, it was obvious they worked well together when they had to. Cooper could see for the first time how they might once have been involved.

"Think about . . . okay, here, Coop," Delilah said. "Think about what it feels like when you tackle someone twice as big as you are. You've certainly done that before, successfully. Only you're doing it in your head instead of with your body."

"Touch can help focus, too," Brent offered. "At least, that's the way your ability seemed to be triggered in the past."

Cooper put a hand on Brent's arm . . . or Margaret's arm, more accurately, even though Samantha was the one they were giving it to.

Thinking too hard about those details was too much for him, so he just set his hand on the slender arm and shut his eyes. Much as he hadn't enjoyed it, he tried to remember what it had felt like when Brent had hijacked his so-called power to try to stop Samantha earlier. Then he tried to recall how he pushed Brent when they first met in the library.

He had been panicked at the time, overwhelmed by those dark memories of the accident that he had tried so hard to keep from surfacing. . . . Memories which, strangely, he had started to be more at peace with since facing them.

Focus, Cooper. The worst you can do is make an ass out of yourself, and it would hardly be the first time you had done that.

He realized he had tightened his grip when Brent let out a small pained sound.

"Sorry," he said, but it was too late. A single, horrid moment came to mind: a car grill meeting a human body. *Human flesh on hot pavement,* Cooper recalled vividly, despite his best efforts not to, *smells like barbecue.*

He heard Samantha let out a sob, and realized that Brent's telepathy must have passed the image on to her.

He *pushed.*

Samantha shouted, *"Wait!"*

He could feel something tearing and struggling. Something cold and dark seemed to lash back at him. Cooper's head reeled and he fell to his knees, retching, beside the bed. Delilah had caught Brent's body, and Cooper heard him moan, then whisper, *"Thank God."*

From the hospital bed came a choked sob.

Holding on to the rail of the bed, Cooper struggled to his feet. He knew instantly that Brent was no longer behind Margaret's brown eyes. Even with her dark brown hair, this was unmistakably Samantha.

"It'll be okay," Cooper told her. "We'll take care of you, and—"

"I remember," she whispered. Then her eyes widened. "Oh, my God, I . . . I remember it all. What I used to be.

What happened." She began narrating the tale with the same horrified expression, as she nervously twisted her short hair between shaking fingertips.

I was a creature of raindrops and mist and power. I was selfless, in that I had never had a "self" to ascribe to myself—no name, no sense of the boundaries of "me" versus the rest of the world, no sense of the passage of time or my passage through it.

I was disturbed by the weeping of a human. Her tears pierced me, though I did not understand why she cried. I did not understand family, much less the loss of such a thing.

I did understand fire, which was the creature that had left her in such a situation, devoid of kin and torn by this pain.

This girl, however, did not just cry. She did not just beckon. She shouted, screamed, and commanded. She used her sorcerer's power, and cast out a net with the intention of snaring another human soul. She did not know the one she called to could not hear her.

I did hear, and though the sorcerer's words meant nothing to me, I could not resist her summons. I might have simply lingered nearby, but I pitied her, and so I accepted the name she called. I think I wanted to speak to her and comfort her.

I was not the only one who responded to her desperate summons. She had not kept enough power to protect herself when the scavengers came.

She screamed, and the sound hurt me. I had allowed her to name me, and so had become aware of "I" and then for the first time I understood pain.

I couldn't let the shadows have her. I fought them, and I yelled at her to go, to run into the forest where I could keep her safe in the mists.

She ran, but she didn't stop. Panicked, she passed beyond the refuge I had offered her, and leaped into danger.

As the first vehicle struck her, the shadows converged. I struggled with them, pulling power from anywhere I could—but so did they. Around us mortals suffered, and every collision of metal and flesh shot through me like the pain was my own.

"I didn't really understand that the body mattered," Samantha said, her gaze focused on a distant memory, her voice hollow. "Margaret's body held on to enough power that even when it should have been torn apart it kept going . . . trying to flee. It crept back into the woods to die, like an animal does, and I tried to pick up the pieces she left behind. Bits of who she was. Bits the shadows didn't get. But I couldn't hold on to it all. I never had memories before. I was overwhelmed. Someone else helped me fight the shadows away, and I held on to him as tightly as I could.

"And then you woke up," she said, looking at Cooper, "and I was Samantha, and that was all." She shivered, and then said, "Ow."

"You might have been immortal, but Margaret's body is still weak," Delilah said. "Your power will probably help it heal and get stronger faster, but for now maybe you should rest a little while?"

"Margaret remembers being hurt," Samantha said. "She broke her ankle when she slipped on a frozen step once. And she sprained her wrist playing . . . oh my *God*."

"What?" Cooper asked, concerned.

When she looked at him next, her wide-eyed expression was the same one the Samantha he had come to know often used.

"I have *friends*," she said. "Or, I mean, Margaret does, but she's me now so I do. I have—*oh*." The sudden elation turned to sorrow, and Cooper didn't need her to say anything more to know she had just remembered that her family was gone.

"Maybe we should leave her alone a while," Delilah suggested. "It might take her some time to work through all of Margaret's memories. She's used to being something without history or emotion or sensation, and now—"

"And now she's human," Cooper interrupted. "You can leave if you want. But if you don't mind, I'll stay with her."

"Yes, please," Samantha said softly. Cooper took her hand, for real this time.

"C'mon, Delilah," Brent said. "I can give you a ride back."

After a moment of hesitation, she replied, "Thanks."

They left together with an uneasy silence hanging between them, which Cooper heard Brent break as they stepped into the hall. "You did good work back there."

"You'd better believe it." Delilah tossed her hair with a laugh. "Though . . . you did, too."

They passed out of earshot, and Cooper's attention returned to Samantha.

A nurse came in to check on them once, and Ryan came

in to let Samantha know that the le Coire family were legal guardians for Margaret and that any necessary medical bills or other expenses would be taken care of, but Samantha just nodded silently to the nurse, and said a quiet thank-you to Ryan.

She spent the rest of the day talking, laughing, and crying. As the evening passed, she seemed to solidify into the girl he had come to know over the summer—just, with a memory of who "she" was.

"I'll have to call my . . . her . . ." She hesitated, and then settled on one. "*My* friends. I don't have any other relatives, but there are some people besides Ryan who would like to know I'm . . . alive." She shook her head. "That's the right thing to do, right? Even if I'm not quite who they knew?"

Cooper nodded. "I changed a lot because of the accident. But my friends still wanted to see me."

"I guess Ryan will let me stay with him, and help me figure out how to use this body. You'll be around, right? I mean, you'll stay in touch?"

"Of course," Cooper assured her. "I wouldn't have gotten through this last summer without you. It's my turn to be here for you now. And I guess I'll still need Ryan's help, too, so I'll be over there a lot."

"Will you take me out to dinner?" Samantha asked, her expression brightening.

"Sure, as soon as Ryan or the doctors say you're up to it," Cooper said.

"No, I mean . . . will you take me *out*?" Samantha said,

the emphasis clear this time, especially when she blushed, and mumbled, "Their mother would have said it's improper for a girl to ask a boy on a date."

Startled, Cooper blurted out, "I guess you owe me dinner, since I'm pretty sure you've watched me shower."

She laughed—and then winced. Her physical recovery would doubtless take a long time.

"Only the once," she replied innocently. She smiled widely. "I'm not going to ask again, Cooper Blake, so as soon as I'm pronounced fit, I expect you to be a gentleman."

Yes, she had watched him shower, teased him mercilessly, hit on him while possessing the body of a friend of his, and was, if he understood it right, not even quite human. Then again, he was a little less than normal himself.

He wasn't an expert on magic or supernatural powers. He couldn't begin to fully comprehend everything he had seen and done recently. But this much was simple. It didn't matter what she was. She was Samantha.

"It's a date," he promised.

ABOUT THE AUTHOR

Amelia Atwater-Rhodes grew up in Concord, Massachusetts. Born in 1984, she wrote her first novel, *In the Forests of the Night,* praised as "remarkable" (*Voice of Youth Advocates*) and "mature and polished" (*Booklist*), when she was thirteen. The other books in the Den of Shadows series are *Demon in My View, Shattered Mirror,* and *Midnight Predator,* all ALA-YALSA Quick Picks for Young Adults. She has also published the five-volume series The Kiesha'ra: *Hawksong,* a *School Library Journal* Best Book of the Year and a *Voice of Youth Advocates* Best Science Fiction, Fantasy, and Horror Selection; *Snakecharm; Falcondance; Wolfcry,* an IRA-CBC Young Adults' Choice; and *Wyvernhail.* Her most recent book was *Persistence of Memory.*

FRANKLIN COUNTY LIBRARY
906 NORTH MAIN STREET
LOUISBURG, NC 27549
BRANCHES IN BUNN.
FRANKLINTON. & YOUNGSVILLE